"I'm Going Along With Your Plan Because You've Given Me No Choice, But I Am Not Sleeping With You, Nathan Reed."

His heavy brows rose in response to her declaration. "I hadn't planned on seducing you." Nate stood up and rounded the coffee table. He leaned over her, trapping her between the long length of his arms.

Annie eased back into the couch, but there wasn't anywhere else to go. She could only breathe in his cologne and remember that same scent on her pillows as she'd slept in this very suite. Back then, Nate had had the ability to play her body like a musical instrument he'd studied his whole life. She'd never been with another man who could bring her pleasure like he had. What they had had was explosive. Mind-blowing.

The closer he came to her, the more she wondered if that connection had severed during their time apart. It didn't feel like it.

His gaze raked over her body. "But if I did...what's so wrong with that? It's not a crime to sleep with your own husband, Annie."

* * *

If you're on Twitter,
tell us what you think of Harlequin Desire!
#harlequindesire

Dear Reader,

Few people know this, since I have been adopted into the Sisterhood of Southern Ladies, but I actually grew up in Las Vegas. I have spent more time in casinos than most tourists could ever dream of. I had my senior prom in Liberace's Mansion (no joke). When I was trying to think of a fun, sexy location for my next book, I thought—why not draw on the city and lifestyle I know best?

Las Vegas is made up of two types of people—the ones who have lived there their whole lives, who grew up in this flashy world and think $4.99 for a prime rib dinner is normal; and the ones who visit, lose all their money and go back to real life. What would happen if these two types of people fell in love? Or worse—eloped at a Vegas wedding chapel? That's where the idea of lifelong Las Vegan Nate and his poker tournament–chasing bride, Annie, came from. Passion would bring them together the first time, but what could possibly reunite them? A little blackmail, perhaps? :)

If you enjoy Nate and Annie's story, tell me by visiting my website, at www.andrealaurence.com, like my fan page on Facebook or follow me on Twitter. I'd love to hear from you!

Enjoy,

Andrea

BACK IN HER HUSBAND'S BED

———

ANDREA LAURENCE

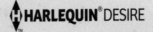

HARLEQUIN® DESIRE

Recycling programs
for this product may
not exist in your area.

ISBN-13: 978-0-373-73297-5

BACK IN HER HUSBAND'S BED

Copyright © 2014 by Andrea Laurence

Printed in U.S.A.

ANDREA LAURENCE

is an award-winning contemporary romance author who has been a lover of books and writing stories since she learned to read. She always dreamed of seeing her work in print and is thrilled to be able to share her books with the world. A dedicated West Coast girl transplanted into the Deep South, she's working on her own "happily ever after" with her boyfriend and five fur-babies. You can contact Andrea at her website: www.andrealaurence.com.

To My Awesome Editor, Shana Smith—

Thank you for rescuing me and this book from the slush pile and seeing us for the diamonds in the (very) rough that we were. Even when this story didn't seem like it would work out, you didn't give up on it or my ability to make it shine. You may not know this, but when you found me, I was on the verge of giving up and I'm so glad I didn't. You have quite literally changed my life and I can't send enough cookies and cupcakes to thank you for it.

One

"Mr. Reed, our facial recognition software has detected a match for the Barracuda in pit three near the dollar slots."

Nate smiled. Like a moth to a flame, Annie had walked right into his trap. He knew she couldn't pass up the chance to play at his poker tournament, even if it meant returning to the scene of the crime. As the owner and manager of the Desert Sapphire Hotel and Casino, it was easy to have Annie red-flagged by his security team. The moment she strolled back in to his casino he knew it.

"We have visual confirmation. She's on her way to the high-roller area." Gabriel Hansen, his chief of security, lifted his hand to his earpiece and listened intently for a moment before nodding in confirmation. "She's joined the Texas Hold'em game with Mr. Nakimori and Mr. Kline."

"Of course she has." Nate set aside his paperwork and made his way to the elevator. There was no time to waste. The Japanese businessman and the oil tycoon had credit lines in the millions, and they'd need every penny if he didn't get down there. They didn't call her the Barracuda for nothing.

"Do you need assistance with this, Mr. Reed?" Gabe was also his best friend, despite the formalities they used at work. Gabe knew what Annie's arrival meant. His offer to accompany him was less about work and more about helping his friend.

Nate sighed and straightened his navy silk tie. He suspected Gabe would relish handcuffing Annie and parading her through the casino so everyone would see. To be honest, he wouldn't mind that himself, but she'd never agree to his plan if he did. "No, I've got this handled."

A quick swipe of his identification card sent the elevator plummeting down the twenty-five floors from his suite to the main casino lobby. A soft chime announced his arrival, and the doors opened to the office corridors where casino operations took place.

The walk through the casino to the high-roller area wasn't long, but each step weighed more heavily on him than the last. Annie was here. In his casino. After three long years. He should be excited to finally confront her. To have his chance to exact his revenge and make her miserable. Or if not excited, perhaps smug. His plan was working just as he'd hoped it would. And yet he was none of those things.

His mouth was dry, his pulse racing in his throat. If he didn't know better, he might think he was nervous. Imagine that: Nathan Reed, millionaire casino owner, former most eligible bachelor in Las Vegas, nervous. It was a ridiculous idea. And yet Annie had always been his weakness.

Nate rounded the corner and spied the entrance to the high-roller lounge. Even across the casino floor, he could spot her. Her back was to him as she leaned over her cards, her legs crossed beneath the table. Her long raven hair spilled over the olive skin of her bare shoulders. Beside her Mr. Nakimori leaned back into his seat, throwing his cards down in disgust.

Nate stopped just behind Annie and placed a heavy hand on her shoulder. She didn't flinch. She'd been expecting him. Game on.

"Gentlemen," he said, flashing a confident smile at the other players at the table and extending a hand to each of them. "It's good to have you both back here at the Sapphire. Is everything going well for you this afternoon?"

Jackson Kline grinned wide and leaned back into his chair. "It was until this pretty little thing showed up. She's taken more of my money than my ex-wife."

Nate smiled and nodded. "Then I'm sure you gentlemen won't mind if I deprive you of her company."

"We're in the middle of a hand."

They were the first words she'd spoken to him since she disappeared. She didn't say "hello." Not even "I'm sorry" or "You're looking well." Just a complaint that he was interrupting her poker hand.

He leaned down and pressed his lips against the soft outer shell of her ear. The smell of her jasmine shampoo filled his lungs as he hovered near. The familiar scent was alluring and reminded him of the tangled sheets she left behind, but he wasn't going to fall prey to her this time. "We need to talk. Fold." The demand was simple and quiet, but powerful.

"Well, gentlemen—" Annie sighed "—I guess I'm done." She slid the cards across the table and reached up to gently extract Nate's hand from her shoulder. He complied, stepping back far enough to allow her to rise from her seat.

"Good afternoon," the men responded in their respective Southern and Japanese accents, although they both seemed visibly relieved to see her go.

Annie grasped her red leather handbag and strolled to the exit with Nate quick on her heels. He moved alongside her, scooping her elbow up with a firm hand and guiding her toward the elevator.

"Take your hands off me," she hissed through gritted teeth. She tugged against his grasp, but it was futile.

Nate couldn't contain a chuckle. "I will not. You and I both know what happened the last time I did that. If you'd prefer, I could have security escort you upstairs instead."

She came to a sudden stop, jerking Nate to turn back to her. Her azure-blue eyes were alight with anger. They penetrated him, a connection forming between them with a sudden snap of electricity. "You wouldn't dare," she said.

God, she was still beautiful. Nate felt the familiar pull in his gut, the heat flooding his groin. The sexual spark had always been there; it was what brought them together. It just couldn't keep them together. It pissed him off that he still reacted to her like this after everything she'd done.

"I wouldn't?" Nate retorted. Annie didn't know him at all. He leaned down, his face inches from hers. "You wanna call my bluff?" Nate didn't wait for an answer but quickly turned and tugged her behind him.

Annie silenced her protests and stopped resisting his pull. He didn't let go until they stepped off the elevator at his suite. She pulled away, turning left toward his office and dropping angrily onto the leather sofa.

"So?" she asked. "You've dragged me up here and cost me a five-thousand-dollar hand. What do you want?"

Nate avoided the couch, opting instead to lean against the large mahogany desk that had once been his grandfather's. He crossed his arms over his chest and took a deep breath. "I have a proposition for you, Barbara Ann."

Annie arched her eyebrow suspiciously at him, obviously not caring for his use of her given name. "You don't have anything I want, Nathan, or my lawyer would've asked for it already."

"That's not true. I can give you the one thing you've wanted for the last three years—a divorce."

Her blue gaze searched his face, probably looking for the catch. "You and your lawyer have been stonewalling the process for years. You've cost me a fortune in legal fees. And now you're just going to wrap it up in a bow and give it to me?"

"Not exactly." Nate smiled and turned to the bar to pour himself a scotch. He'd let her stew awhile and prolong the torture. She'd made him wait long enough. "Drink?" he offered with his glass held up, more out of politeness than a desire to be truly hospitable.

"You know I don't drink."

Nate stiffened. He'd forgotten. She hated the way alcohol made her feel out of control. It was amazing how the details could slip your mind when you were apart. What else had he forgotten? "A soda, then? Water?"

"No, I'm fine, thank you."

Nate dropped ice cubes into his own glass and nodded before pouring the golden liquid over it. "Very well." He took a sip, appreciating the warm sensation it lit in his stomach. It fueled his resolve and distracted him from the pangs of lust he was determined to ignore.

It was getting harder every minute he spent with her. There was something about Annie that made his blood sing. It was more than just her exotic beauty or her shrewd intelligence. He could still feel the silky slide of her ebony hair across his bare chest as she hovered over him. The musical sound of her laughter. All together it was an intoxicating combination. Just being around her again was enough to ignite the flames of his desire.

And then he would remember that she wanted a divorce. That she had left him in the night after less than two weeks of marriage without a word until he was served the papers.

He supposed he should be grateful that Annie had bothered to file for divorce. His mother hadn't gone to the trouble. She'd just disappeared and sent his father into a spiral of depression that nearly destroyed the Desert Sapphire and his grandfather's legacy with it. Nate was stronger than that. He'd rebuilt the hotel and helped transform the industry, even as she'd left him. He wasn't about to be broken by a woman.

Even one as breathtaking as Annie.

She watched him warily from her seat as he walked toward her and leisurely sipped his drink. "I know you haven't had a sudden change of heart. So what's going on?"

He certainly hadn't. Honestly, it pained him to finally give her what she wanted, but the tournament was more important. The organization that sponsored the most prestigious poker tournament in the industry had a long-standing agreement with another casino. To lure them to the Desert Sapphire, it had taken him three years and a few promises he needed Annie to help him keep.

"I am working on a side project of sorts during the tournament and you're just the right person for the job." He paused, sipping his scotch thoughtfully. "If I sign the papers and give you the divorce you want, you agree to help me."

"I don't understand. How could I possibly—"

Nate cut her protest short with a wave of his hand. "I'm sure you've heard about the cheating problem the poker circuit is having. The rumors are getting fairly loud and the tournament sponsor's reputation is suffering for it. Everyone is anticipating they'll hit the tournament."

Annie sighed. "There's always rumors of cheating, but nothing ever comes of it. The people they catch are usually small potatoes compared to the amount of money exchanged in one of these events. What's the big deal?"

"Hosting the tournament is a huge draw for my hotel. As you well know, it's been held at the Tangiers for the last twenty years. Talking the organizers into moving it here had taken more than some nice negotiating. They wanted concrete guarantees that anyone cheating during the tournament would be caught and prosecuted, to send a message to the community."

"And why are they so confident that your team can do a better job than the Tangiers?"

"Because I have one of the best security systems in the business, with some of the most qualified staff you can hire. We go well beyond the typical measures most casinos employ."

"Seems like overkill to me. I hardly think you can stop cheating."

"This hotel was on the verge of going under when I took over from my father. He wasn't well at the time and people took advantage of the situation. Our biggest issue was people gaming the house, especially our own employees. I wouldn't tolerate that on my watch and invested in cutting-edge technology to stop it. Over the last five years, our estimated losses from cheating are down by eighty percent."

"Then why do you need me?" Annie crossed her arms defensively, pressing her breasts tight against the low V-cut of her sleeveless red silk top.

Just a quick glance at the soft curves of her femininity sent a sharp spike of need down his spine and forced him to turn away. "Because," he said, "I suspect this is a more elaborate and well-organized operation than we're used to. More people are involved…new faces with clean records. But we have to succeed. If we manage to bust this ring, I've got a guaranteed ten-year contract for the tournament. That's something my grandfather wouldn't have even hoped for."

"And what?" she prompted. "You think I know who's involved?"

"I think you probably have your suspicions. You've been active in the community for several years and have to have heard your share of stories." He lifted his gaze to meet hers. "I also think you could flush them out with the right…*motivation*."

Annie leaped up from her seat, the nervous energy his proposal generated propelling her off the leather couch. "I'm not a snitch." There was no way she was going to ruin her reputation like that. Not for a divorce, not for the attentions of a charming, handsome man like Nate. Her honor was all she had in this business.

"If we do it right, no one will ever know that you are."

"And how's that? There are cameras everywhere. The odds are they have help on the inside, possibly even your own security guys and dealers. You don't think they'll notice us talking?"

"Nope. They won't."

He hadn't told her everything. Her game was poker, but Nate's game was chess. He was already three moves ahead of her. Annie hated being outmaneuvered. "Enlighten me."

His mouth curved up in a sly smile. "There are no cameras in here."

Annie looked around the office and down the dark corridor to his suite. She sincerely hoped not. They would've gotten an eyeful during their wedding night. "And no one will find it suspicious that I'm up in your suite? That I'm spending all my time with the casino boss?"

"Why shouldn't you spend time with *your husband?*"

Annie's blood turned to ice in her veins. If there was one thing she clung to, it was that no one knew about their mistake. Their marriage had been a secret she'd shared only with her sister, Tessa, and her mother. Yes, she and Nate would've told people eventually, but in the beginning they'd been far too wrapped up in one another to share the good news. Then it was over. "You don't think people will question that we're suddenly married? That we're together again after all this time apart?"

Nate shrugged. "We'll just tell the truth. We got married three years ago. It didn't work out. We separated. You came back for the tournament and we reconciled."

"That's not the truth."

"No, but the best lies have a good bit of truth in them. The paper trail will back up our story. And we won't give them any reason to doubt it." He smiled a wide, confident smile that started to melt her defenses away before she could think through his statement.

No reason to doubt they were married? "You…you don't honestly expect us to…?" The air in the room suddenly seemed cooler, her skin contracting with goose bumps. Annie crossed her arms protectively over her chest and ran her hands over the bumpy flesh of her bare upper arms.

"No—" he laughed "—of course not. It will just be for show. You'll need to stay here in the suite with me. We'll eat together in public, be affectionate. You might have to suffer through a few of my kisses so any time we spend alone will be chalked up to romantic interludes. No one will suspect what we're really doing together."

Annie felt the rush of blood rise to her cheeks and chase away the chill. When was the last time she'd blushed? Probably her first kiss in sixth grade. She learned to master her emotions not long after that. It made her an excellent poker player. It also made her a really crappy girlfriend. Or wife, as the case was here. Somehow Nate was the only one able to put a dent in her armor.

Suffering wasn't exactly the response she had to his kisses. They always made her head swim. Made her thoughts turn to mush and her body into a bundle of raw nerves. His kisses had been enough to convince her that getting married after only a few days together was a good idea. If Annie was going to kiss him, she'd have to be very careful. The phrase *one thing leads to another* had never been truer than with Nate.

This was a bad idea all around. Spying on her fellow players? Acting the happy couple with Nate? That was like playing with fire. No. This was a ridiculous suggestion. She wouldn't be a party to Nate's games. "What if I say no?"

Annie watched her estranged husband take a large sip of his scotch and cross his arms over his chest. His expensive gray suit coat strained against his broad shoulders as he leaned casually against his desk. He didn't seem at all affected by their conversation or the thought of kissing her. Apparently Annie was the only one still afflicted with that weakness. He was only interested in using her to make his precious hotel even more successful.

Despite everything, she remembered why she'd fallen for Nate. He was all that she was supposed to want in a man: tall, handsome, strong, intelligent, caring and exceedingly wealthy. What she didn't know was how to breathe when someone held her so tightly. She wasn't used to someone else having a say in what she could or couldn't do. Nate's expectations of his wife had been more than she could handle.

The women in her family weren't known for keeping men around. Her marriage, as short-lived as it might've been, was the first in several generations. Magdala Baracas had taught her daughters early on that men could be amusing, but in the end, they were more trouble than they were worth. And looking at her "husband" now just reinforced her mother's wisdom. Nate was infuriating. She'd filed for divorce and he'd contested, refusing to finalize the agreement just to punish her. Now he dangled her freedom as a carrot, but the price was too high.

Nate pinned her with his dark gaze. "No cooperation, no divorce. Simple as that."

Uncomfortable, she shifted her glance away, tracing the angles of his smooth jaw to the dark blond curls that hung just at the edge of his shirt collar. His hair was longer than she remembered. She liked it better this way. Not that it mattered anymore what she thought. Despite what the law said, Nate wasn't hers and hadn't been for a very long time.

Annie sighed in frustration but refused to just bite at whatever he dangled in front of her. "Come on, Nathan, be honest. This isn't about poker cheats. This is about bending me to your will and punishing me for leaving you. You couldn't possibly want to be married to me after everything that's happened."

Annie couldn't tell if her rambling was helping or hurting her cause, but she couldn't stop the words from gushing out of her after three years of silence. "I regret that we confused lust and love and got into this mess. But I want to close this chapter of my life and move on. I don't want to play these games anymore. Please."

At that, Nate took a step away, a Cheshire-cat grin crossing his face. The sudden shift in his mood was unnerving. The dimple in his cheek she'd kissed a hundred times was barely visible from where she was standing. "Did you really think it would be that easy? That you could just look at me with those big blue eyes and I would change my mind?"

Annie stiffened. No, but she wanted this over. Done. She didn't need a single reason to have to be in the same room with Nate again. It was too dangerous. She was too weak. The farther they were apart, the firmer her resolve.

"What's your lawyer charge by the hour, Annie? If you turn down my offer, we can see who runs out of money first."

That was certainly a losing game for her, even after a few fabulously lucrative years. Annie flopped back against the couch, unable to continue fighting with him. "Please, Nate." She wanted out of the marriage, but she knew she couldn't win this hand. She gazed down into her lap. "I can't change what happened between us in the past. But don't force me to jeopardize my future. If someone finds out I'm spying for you, my career will be ruined. I will be the most hated woman in poker."

Annie didn't look up but caught Nate's movement out of the corner of her eye as he settled into a nearby chair. She couldn't say anything else. She'd laid all her cards on the table, but the dispassionate look in Nate's dark eyes told her it wouldn't matter. Whether in court or in the casino, Nate would ruin her and have his revenge. After three years, he had her right where he wanted her.

"These are my terms," he said, his voice cold. "Do you want a divorce or not?"

Of course she did. But… She shook her head. "This is blackmail."

Nate smiled widely, his pleasure at watching her squirm plainly evident. "*Blackmail* is such a dirty word. I prefer to look at it as a mutually beneficial arrangement. I catch my cheaters and secure the tournament for a decade. You get your divorce without going bankrupt first. Simple as that."

That was a vast understatement. It couldn't be more complicated. "Why me?"

Nate watched her, his lips pursing in thought before he spoke. "I need an insider. You're an excellent player. You have a good read of your competitors. The odds of you making it to the final table are in our favor. And I have the leverage to incentivize you. It's perfect."

Not entirely perfect. She took a deep breath and squeezed her eyes tightly shut for a moment before she spoke. She wanted to walk away from the Desert Sapphire when the tournament was done and never have a reason to see Nathan Reed again. And yet the price was high. Spying for him. Publicly adoring him. Privately conspiring under the guise of their so-called marriage. It was dangerous territory. But the tournament was only a week long. If all went well, she could play poker as planned, throw Nate a couple leads to chase and hopefully walk away from the Sapphire a free woman.

"And I can trust you to keep your word if I keep up my end of the bargain?"

Nate arched an eyebrow. "Annie, *my* trustworthiness has never been in question. But yes. If you agree to see this through, I'll call my lawyer and have him withdraw the protest. If we get things started soon, the divorce should be finalized in a few weeks' time."

He'd left her no other choice. She met his gaze across the coffee table. "All right, Nate. You've got a deal."

Two

Annie regretted the words the minute they passed her lips, but she couldn't take it back now.

Nate glared at her in disbelief. It was obvious he'd been prepared for a battle. He thought she'd fight harder. There was a flicker of disappointment across his face as he straightened up in his chair and mentally regrouped.

Annie hated that she was so aware of his body. Every twitch of every muscle beneath the tight fabric of his suit registered in her mind. She could tell herself that she was just good at reading body language after years of poker, but it wasn't true. She knew him better than she cared to admit. Her own body remembered every inch of the hard physique hidden under those expensive suits. It wasn't something she could easily forget.

"Well, good," Nate finally managed to say. "I'm glad you could be reasonable about this." He set his glass onto the table and nodded. "Have you checked in to the hotel?"

She hadn't bothered. She'd figured Nate would have his security goons come after her before she could reach her room. She'd arrived a day early to get that unpleasantness out of the way so she could focus on her game. "No. Not yet. I wanted to play a little first."

"Okay, I'll radio to have your bags brought upstairs. I assume you left them with the bellhop?"

Annie opened her mouth to argue, but he was already barking orders into a push-to-talk cell phone at his hip. He'd told her she would stay with him as part of the cover. Somehow she hadn't let her mind process that part of the deal yet.

Her mind raced, thinking of the private suite that sat dark and quiet down the corridor. Nate owned a home in Henderson, but she knew he usually stayed at the Sapphire when he was working, which was all the time. As she could recall, there was a full kitchen, living and dining rooms...but only one bed.

She frowned, kicking herself for not getting all the details before agreeing to this. Now she had no negotiating power at all. "Where will I sleep?"

"The bedroom." Nate said the words as though it were the most obvious answer in the world.

Nate's gaze had been cool and detached since the moment they got upstairs. He was obviously more interested in power and revenge than seduction, but even then she wasn't comfortable with the idea. "And what about you?" she pressed. There. That should be clear enough.

Nate's lips twisted in a faint grin. "I don't sleep, remember?"

That was almost true. He did have the ability to make it on only three or four hours of sleep a night, but he *did* sleep. "You sleep enough."

This time he grinned wide, his perfectly aligned smile blazing white against his tanned skin. "We'll worry about that when the time comes."

The smile was not enough to charm her. He was being deliberately evasive. She glanced down at her watch. It was after seven. She was a night owl, but even then the time was coming sooner rather than later. "I'm going along with your plan because you've given me no choice, but I am *not* sleeping with you, Nathan Reed."

His heavy brows rose in response to her declaration. "I hadn't planned on seducing you." Nate stood up and rounded the coffee table. He leaned over her, trapping her between the long lengths of his arms.

Annie eased back into the couch, but there wasn't anywhere else to go. She could only breathe in his cologne and remember that same scent on her pillows as she slept in this very suite. Back then, Nate had the ability to play her body like a musical instrument he'd studied his whole life. She'd never been with another man who could bring her pleasure like he had. What they had was explosive. Mind-blowing.

The closer he came to her, the more she wondered if that connection had severed during their time apart. It didn't feel like it.

His gaze raked over her body. "But if I did…what's so wrong with that? It's not a crime to sleep with your own husband, Annie."

She felt a surge of electricity run through her body when he spoke her name. He'd said it the way he had in the past, with the low, soft tones she remembered him whispering into her ear as they made love. Whatever it was between them was still there. For her, at least. She couldn't even respond with him so close.

"Besides," he continued, "I don't seem to recall you complaining much about it before."

Her mouth suddenly felt dry. Annie ran her tongue quickly across her bottom lip. Even after all this time, she still wanted him. There was no question of it. "That was a long time ago," she said, her voice a little too breathy to ring true even to her own ears.

"We'll see about that." Nate stood up, pulling away from her and breaking the spell. Annie felt him take all the oxygen in the room with him as he stepped back and scooped his drink off the table. He took a sip, the ice clinking in the mostly empty glass, and turned his back to her. He was as calm and unaffected as he would be conducting a business deal.

Then she understood. She was right; this wasn't just about busting cheaters in his casino. There were other ways to go about catching them that didn't require them to pose as the married couple they were. Methods that didn't make him touching her necessary for their cover.

No, Nate wanted to make her pay. To get the small sense of justice he'd been lacking for the past three years. She couldn't exactly call it torture, but he would be using every weapon in his arsenal—from seduction to indifference—to ensure she was uneasy and off her game. She would get her divorce, but the next week would be anything but simple. The odds were she could kiss this tournament win goodbye. Her focus was already shattered and it hadn't even begun.

The chime of the elevator startled her. Annie looked over to see Gabe, the head of security, enter the foyer with her luggage. He was one of the only people with the card to access Nate's private suite.

Annie stood and rounded the coffee table to approach him, but his gaze stopped her cold. Gabe had always had a smile and a laugh for her, but not today. His hazel eyes were like knives, shooting sharp accusations at her from across the room. His jaw was tight, the muscles in his thick neck tense. There was more anger in Gabe than she'd seen in Nate. Perhaps Nate was simply better at controlling it.

Gabe turned toward the darkened suite without speaking and dropped her luggage carelessly beside the dining room table. "Call me if you need me, sir." He said the words while looking at Annie, the threat inherent. A moment later, the elevator doors reopened and he disappeared.

With him gone the heavy weight of his anger suddenly lifted from her chest. Annie had never realized how protective Gabe was of Nate. She bet if given the chance, he'd shoot her with his Taser just to watch her twitch.

Annie chewed her bottom lip thoughtfully. Of course he was angry. He'd been there every day of the past three years. He was probably the one who'd gotten Nate drunk and hauled him to a strip club to get over her. As a friend and as a security officer, he obviously disapproved of Nate's plan to use Annie in the sting operation. Especially the part about them living together. Gabe could see the potential problems a mile away.

To tell the truth, Annie wasn't entirely thrilled with that part of the plan, either. She wanted to follow him downstairs, to tell him she had no intention of getting involved with Nate again, but knew it wouldn't help. Annie turned around, stopping short when she found Nate smiling. It was the first sincere grin he'd cracked since she arrived and of course, it was at her discomfort.

"He's not your biggest fan."

"I gathered that much. I'd hoped you hadn't told anyone about us. Does anyone else know? Should I watch for flying daggers from housekeeping?"

Nate laughed and shook his head. "No, just Gabe. I wasn't even going to tell him, but he found your wedding ring."

The ring. Annie had forgotten. She'd left her platinum wedding band on the bedside stand. She hadn't felt good about taking it. Leaving had been the right thing to do, but taking the ring so soon after receiving it felt like stealing.

She watched, stunned, as Nate twisted a tiny band from his pinky finger and held it out to her. "You'll need this back. For the cover," he added.

Annie took the tiny silver loop from his hand and examined it like a lost artifact. It was a dull, brushed-platinum band with shiny accents around the edge. They'd picked the rings out in such a hurry. At that moment, all she'd wanted was to be Mrs. Nathan Reed. *What the hell had she been thinking?*

"Why are you wearing it?" she asked.

"I wear it as a reminder."

Annie got the distinct impression that he didn't mean it in a sentimental way. More a daily reminder of how much she'd suffer if he got his hands on her again. "Where's *your* ring?"

"Put away. I couldn't very well wear mine and tarnish my reputation as Vegas's most eligible bachelor." He said the last word with audible distaste before he walked around his desk, fished in the top drawer and pulled out a small black velvet box.

"I can see how being married might interfere with your social agenda."

Nate looked up, studying her face for a moment before opening the box and slipping the matching ring onto his left hand. He stretched his fingers out, testing the feel of the long-forgotten jewelry before making a fist. A slight frown pulled down the corners of his mouth when he spoke. "I have no social agenda, Annie. I thought that was one of the reasons you decided to leave me."

"No, I..." Annie's voice trailed off midprotest. She didn't really want to talk about why she left. Not now. It wouldn't change anything. What was done was done and their agreement would close the door on the past for good. Her gaze dropped down to the ring in her hand before her fingers closed over it.

Nate's brow furrowed, his eyes focused on her tightly clenched fist. "Put on the ring," he demanded softly.

Her heart skipped a beat in her chest. She'd sooner slip a noose over her head. That's how it felt, at least. Even back then. When she'd woken up the morning after the wedding with the platinum manacle clamped onto her, she'd popped a Xanax to stop the impending panic attack. She'd convinced herself that it would be okay, it was just the nerves of a new bride, but it hadn't taken long to realize she'd made a mistake.

Annie scrambled to find a reason not to put the ring on. She couldn't afford to start hyperventilating and give Nate the upper hand in any of this. "I thought I might wait until I had a chance to clean it. Give it a good polish."

It was stupid and she knew it. Why did putting on a ring symbolic of nothing but a legally binding slip of paper bother her so much? The smothering sensation was growing more oppressive, like a steamy, wet blanket draped over her face on a smolderingly hot Miami day. It was just how she'd felt back then. Why she'd had to run.

Nate frowned. He moved across the room with the stealthy grace of a panther, stopping just in front of her. Without speaking, he reached out and gripped her fist. One by one, he pried her fingers back and took the band from her.

She was no match for his firm grasp, especially when the surprising tingle of awareness traveled up her arm at his touch. He held her left hand immobile, her heart pounding rapidly in her chest as the ring moved closer and closer.

"May I, Mrs. Reed?"

Her heart stopped altogether at the mention of her married name. Annie's breath caught in her throat as he pushed the band over her knuckle and nestled it snugly in place, as he had at their wedding. His hot touch was in vast contrast to the icy-cold metal against her skin. Although it fit perfectly, the ring seemed too tight. So did her shoes. On second thought, everything felt too tight. The room was too small. The air was too thin.

Annie's brain started swirling in the fog overtaking her mind. She started to tell Nate she needed to sit down, but it was too late.

Nate was enjoying watching Annie squirm up until the moment her eyes rolled into her head. He moved on reflex, catching her slumping body in his arms. He quickly repositioned his hold and lifted her up, carrying her down the hall to the bedroom. He settled her onto the navy comforter covering his king-size bed and sat down on the edge beside her.

Annie had lingered on his mind since the day she left. Bringing her to her knees before giving her the divorce she wanted was a surefire way to put her out of his thoughts for good. Catching a couple cheaters and guaranteeing the success of his hotel for years to come was a great way to make her earn her freedom. And she made it too easy, really. He knew all the right buttons to push. He was pleasantly surprised at how gratifying it had been so far.

At least until she passed out.

Nate leaned over her. Annie's breathing had returned to normal. Her ruby lips parted, and her anxious expression faded as her body relaxed into the plush mattress.

Nate couldn't help reaching out and running a finger along the blush of her cheek. Her skin was as soft as he remembered, like silk. She sighed as the back of his hand slid down her face and along her jaw.

The Annie the public saw was always so cool, so put together. He'd watched her on televised tournaments over the years and seen her in interviews. She was unshakable. Unflappable. Nothing like the wildly passionate woman who had shared his bed. Or the one who passed out cold at the idea of wearing her wedding ring.

She stirred so many emotions in him. Anger, jealousy, arousal, resentment, anxiety… Being around her now was like riding the roller coaster across the street. He was an even-keeled guy. A levelheaded businessman. That made it even more irritating knowing she could impact him the way no other woman had. He just hoped he could keep it all inside.

When she'd first left, he was confused and furious. His worst fears had been realized. It was as though his mother had abandoned him all over again. He had watched his father crumble under the weight of his grief. The only thing Nate knew for certain was that he wouldn't let Annie break him. He'd funneled his anger into building the greatest damn casino in Las Vegas and finding the perfect way to exact his revenge.

Yes, they might have rushed to the altar. Yes, they might have had little more than fantastic sex in common. But their marriage would end on his terms, not hers. She'd forfeited her vote when she walked out. Now that he had her back here, bending to his will, he would finally be able to put her, and them, behind him.

Perhaps. As he looked down at the beautiful, exciting woman…his wife…he began to wonder if luring her back here with the tournament was a mistake. The vengeance surging through his veins had dulled, leaving only the desire to possess her once again.

Back then, his need for Annie had been all consuming. Nate hadn't wanted to let her out of his bed, much less his life. Marrying her had seemed like the best way to guarantee that Annie would be his forever. The irony was that it was the marriage itself that drove her away. Everything had been perfect before then.

Annie groaned softly, her eyes fluttering a moment before opening. She looked around the room in confusion before her sapphire gaze met his. "What happened?"

"You fainted. Apparently the mere thought of people knowing you were married to me was too much for you to take." He didn't bother to mask the irritation in his voice.

"What am I...?" She looked around again, the crease between her eyebrows deepening in thought. "Why am I lying in your bedroom?"

Nate smiled down at her. "*Our* bedroom, sweetheart. Like a gentleman, I carried you in here when you fainted. Anyway, I'm surprised you recognize the place. I'd have thought you blocked it from your memory with the rest of our marriage."

Annie frowned and pushed herself up onto her elbows. "Nate, the problems in our relationship had nothing to do with this room. The bedroom was the *only* place it worked."

She sat up and slowly inched off the foot of the bed. Pulling herself together, she quickly tugged down her fitted black skirt and smoothed her red top. Her expression hardened, her emotions unreadable. Within seconds, the Annie of the past was gone and *the Barracuda* had returned. He was glad. The cool, calm poker player was far easier for Nate to resist.

Annie left the room and returned with her two bags. "Where can I put my things?"

The large, red Louis Vuitton roller and toiletry bag

were just the right size for a woman on the move all the time. After she left, Nate had hired a private detective to find out more about his elusive bride. He'd told Nate that although Annie had a sparsely decorated condo in Miami, she was almost never there. She roamed from one tournament to the next, living in hotels out of these red bags.

As someone who had practically grown up in the same building he stood in right now, he couldn't understand her wanderlust. He'd known she traveled to the various tournaments to compete, but somehow he'd thought that marrying him would give her a reason to settle in one place. That her love of the game would give her an interest in helping him build up the Sapphire, working side by side as partners. He had been wrong.

Nate opened the door to the walk-in closet and moved some clothes to the opposite side. "You can hang up your things here. If you need any more space, just slide my stuff over."

Annie nodded stiffly and pushed past him to the closet. He took a few steps back to linger in the doorway and watch as she slowly unpacked. She was methodical as she unzipped the bag and carefully removed each piece. It was like a ritual she'd repeated a thousand times. How had he ever thought he could get her to unpack for good?

"If you have what you need, I'm going downstairs. I'll see you for dinner at Carolina's at eight-thirty. Be prepared for our first public outing as husband and wife."

At that, he turned on his heel and marched down the hallway to the elevator. He didn't wait for her response. He needed to get away from her for a while. To take a deep breath that wasn't warm with her scent. To clear his mind and replan his strategy. His stomach couldn't take the never-ending swing of the emotional pendulum being around her brought on. Wanting her and then despising

her. Remembering every inch of her body and then realizing he didn't know a damn thing about her.

Once downstairs, he marched through the casino for
his standing meeting with Gabe and Jerry Moore, his
casino floor manager. They met in the Pit Three lounge,
where they would catch him up on the hotel activities.
Tonight, he would also get a drink. He normally wouldn't
drink while working, but all bets were off the moment
Annie walked into his casino. He needed something to
dull his thoughts, to fend off the building arousal. Not
to get drunk—he couldn't trust himself not to do something stupid—just enough to numb.

By the time he reached the lounge, Gabe and Jerry
were already seated in the back corner booth. They went
on easily with their normal routines from there. Gabe re-
ported on any incidents worth mentioning, provided the
latest security codes and gave him the access card for
Annie. Jerry rattled on for a while about a couple high
rollers and preparation for the tournament.

The tournament was not an easy event to arrange.
Nate was happy to sip on his vodka tonic and give his
mind over to the intricacies. A portion of the casino floor
had already been roped off and tables rearranged. The
kickoff cocktail party was under control. Patricia in the
public relations office had been in contact with the event
sponsors and working with ESPN for the past few weeks.
Everything seemed to be going well.

His years of hard work really had paid off. Nate had
fought hard to bring the hotel back after his father's neg-
ligent management. Now it was clear that his dedication
and work ethic had rubbed off on his staff. The people he
hired were inspired to make the Desert Sapphire the most
successful hotel-casino in Las Vegas. His grandfather
would be proud of what Nate had made of his life's work.

"So is everything in place in terms of the *arrangement* with Annie?" Gabe asked, drawing Nate back into the conversation he'd been having alone with Jerry.

Nate noted his tone. Gabe didn't like his plan at all and made no secret of it. "Yes. I think with her assistance we will have a very good shot of putting an end to this and securing the tournament contract."

Jerry nodded in approval. His casino manager had worked at the Sapphire for thirty years, helping Nate's grandfather start the place. After a heart attack and an unfulfilling decade of retirement, he'd come back to help his best friend's grandson. The whole Annie situation had happened during his hiatus.

"Remind me again of the story we're using?" Jerry ran his wrinkled hand over the balding dome of his head. "I want to make sure when people ask, I'm telling it right."

Nate repeated their cover for everyone's benefit. "Annie and I got married a couple years ago, but it didn't work out. She came back for the tournament and we've reconciled. I'd leave it at that. Too many details and we run the risk of messing up."

Jerry's radio squawked at his hip. He lifted it to his ear to listen to the message before responding and turning to Nate. "If we're done here, I need to get over to pit one."

Nate dismissed him with a wave of his hand and then watched the older man shuffle out of the lounge. He hoped he had half that much spunk when he was in his seventies.

Turning back, Nate could tell Gabe was biting his tongue. He wasn't happy, idly rotating a cardboard coaster on the table and glaring at the platinum band on Nate's ring finger. "Just say it, Gabe."

Gabe shook his head, his closely cropped goatee emphasizing his frown. "I just don't like this. I don't trust her. How do we know she isn't friends with one of the cheaters? She could tip them off or send us on a wild goose chase. We have no idea where her loyalty lies. Hell, she could be in on it herself."

Nate doubted that. Annie had too much pride in her skills. But Gabe was right about her loyalties. She'd been in the game a long time, knew everyone. If it wasn't for the divorce papers he was dangling, he couldn't be sure. "She wants a divorce. Her loyalty to herself will trump everything else."

"I know why this is important for the hotel, but why her?"

"Why not use Annie? She owes me after all this time. If I can make her miserable and teach her a lesson this week, all the better. Once the tournament is over, I'll let her walk away and never give her a second thought."

"For someone who says he doesn't care about a woman," Gabe commented dryly, "you're sure putting a lot of time and effort into this."

"I deserve my chance to get back at her, don't I?"

"Sure. She deserves everything you'll dish out and then some. I just worry this isn't going to end well."

Nate appreciated Gabe's concern but wished his friend had more faith in him. "It will all go as planned. We will bust those dirty crooks, Annie will pay for her irresponsible and thoughtless actions, and I'll finally have some peace."

"I've seen the way you look at her, Nate. Even today. It's still there. It may not be love, but whatever it is was strong enough for you two to lose your minds and elope after a few days together." Gabe paused, leaning across the table toward him. "If she's your sexual kryptonite, what do you think will happen living in such close proximity for over a week?"

Nate could handle Annie. "Nothing is going to happen. I've learned my lesson, I assure you."

Three

After Nate left, Annie finished unpacking and found herself at a loss for what to do. Her day had taken a radical turn since Nate interrupted her game, and she had far too much nervous energy running through her veins. The situation was nerve-racking, but Nate made it even worse. As usual, he'd managed to stir her suppressed arousal and send her libido into overdrive.

She had an hour before dinner, so she opted for a hot shower and some fresh clothes. It had been a long flight from Miami.

By the time she rounded the corner to the entrance of Carolina's Restaurant, it was eight-thirty on the nose. The dark, romantic steak house was the jewel of the hotel's restaurants. There was always an extensive waiting list for those wanting to propose or celebrate an anniversary. Nate and Annie had eaten there only once. It was here, among the candlelight and low, sultry music, that the idea of eloping had been conceived.

Nate, ever punctual, was standing there waiting for her. He was preoccupied with his smartphone, typing something with his right thumb while his left hand anxiously jingled the keys and change in his pocket.

Annie lingered, taking a moment to watch him while he was distracted. He typed for a few seconds and then laughed, scrolling with his thumb and shaking his head. This Nate was more like the man she remembered. His cocky, businessman veneer had been in place when he spoke to her earlier today. He'd constructed pretty high walls since she left. Annie didn't blame him—she'd given him the bricks to build it—but she did miss the thoughtful, charming man she'd fallen for.

She'd never tell him the truth, but she had been completely consumed by her attraction to Nate. Part of her still cared about him. It just didn't change her decision. It had all been too much, too fast.

Maybe it was her roaming Gypsy blood that kept her from settling down. Maybe it was her fiercely independent streak that wouldn't stand for a man trying to control her. Annie didn't know. But the first time Nate had scoffed at the idea of her traveling to a tournament, she could feel the constrictive hold choking her.

Nate slipped the phone into his pocket and looked down at his watch impatiently. She couldn't run this time if she ever wanted her freedom back. It was time to be man and wife for the crowds. Annie took a deep breath and prepared to begin her performance.

"Hey, there, sexy." Annie spoke loudly enough for those around them to hear as she strode quickly to him. Before he could react, she snaked a hand around his neck and tugged him down into a hello kiss.

She had every intention of making it a quick peck for show, but once their lips touched, something stronger than she was held her there. Annie remembered the feeling... The sensation from her past that had nearly ruined her. She could feel the live current running through her body, every nerve awakened after years of dormancy.

When the initial shock of her assault wore off, Nate did his part, wrapping his arms around her and pulling her against him. His mouth molded to her lips, just as her every curve did to his hard, angular body. They matched perfectly. It was such a natural feeling. It was how she imagined coming home would feel if she had one.

It was only this thought that propelled her to pull away and push gently against the lapels of his dark gray Armani suit. This wasn't home. This was a ruse. Nothing more.

Nate released her lips but kept her body still and close. "Well, hello," he whispered low, one eyebrow curiously raised at her.

"Hello," Annie responded, her voice weak with her own shallow, rapid breathing. She didn't want him to know she still responded to him like this. Quickly, she searched for the words to convince them both it was only a part of the cover. "Was that convincing enough?"

Nate's dark eyes searched her face for a moment before he frowned slightly and released his grip on her waist. "Yes, quite. I see you've dedicated yourself to your new role." His voice had returned to the polite and formal.

Annie smiled sweetly and took his arm as he offered it. "I'm absolutely starving," she said, effectively changing the subject.

"I hope so. I've had Leo reserve a very romantic and very—" he leaned in to add the last part quietly "—*public* table for us." They bypassed the crowd waiting to be seated and Nate gave a quick wave to Leo, the maître d'.

"Good evening, Mr. Reed. Your table is ready for you and Mrs. Reed." The tall, thin Asian man grabbed two menus and led them through the restaurant to a candlelit table for two in the center of the room. Leo pulled out Annie's chair and seated her, placing both their napkins and providing the menu with the night's selections. "Enjoy your meal and congratulations to you both."

When Leo disappeared, Annie felt the sudden weight of being alone with Nate in such a romantic setting. The first time they'd eaten there, he'd reserved a cozy table in a dark corner so they wouldn't be disturbed. Now, although the table was still quite nice, it was out in the open where everyone would see them together. And apparently, the word was out about their marriage. Leo knew. It wouldn't take long to spread.

Nate reached across the table and took Annie's hand. She had to remember not to jerk away and instead leaned into him.

"You know, you did a very good job just now. Fooled even me for a moment," he began, his voice soft as velvet. "Makes me feel better for falling for it last time. Sometimes I forget you're a professional liar."

Annie tried to tug away from him, but his iron grasp held her tight. He glanced down at her hand, ignoring her quiet groans of protest. "You really need a manicure." He murmured the casual insult like a lover's words in her ear and released her.

She forced a smile, gently untangling her fingers to take a sip of her water. "Well, it's hard to keep up with the little things when you're like me, always on the run."

"Indeed." His dark eyes pierced her as sharply as his words, although the rest of his face and body language oozed nothing but adoration. She wasn't the only one that excelled in deception. "I'll send Julia up to the suite tonight. She works in the hotel salon."

"That won't be necessary. I'll make a point of going to see her instead. The less time I spend in that suite, the better."

Nate smiled wide. "You'll have to sleep in that bed eventually, Annie."

"Not while you're in it," she snapped.

Their server interrupted at that exact moment, introducing herself as Renee and ending their argument. She had a basket of warm, crusty bread and herb butter. "Good evening, Mr. Reed. Mrs. Reed," she said with a grin. Everyone seemed exceedingly pleased about their boss's big news. It was quite the little family here at the Sapphire.

Renee continued on about the fresh catch of the day, but Annie didn't pay very much attention. She was focused entirely on Nate. He was still glaring at her under his blond lashes, despite appearing to look down at the menu with interest. In the past, his glance could send shivers of anticipation up her spine. At the moment, it made her skin crawl. He was surveying her the way she would another player at the poker table. Reading weaknesses. Judging their reactions.

She didn't like it one bit.

"Champagne, I think. We're celebrating tonight."

The single word snapped Annie out of her thoughts. *Champagne?* She watched Renee disappear around the corner. "You know I don't drink."

Nate took a deep breath, fighting to maintain the look of adoration on his face. "Smile, sweetheart. You do tonight. We have to celebrate our reconciliation. Normal people would order champagne."

"I didn't drink champagne when we married. Why would I do it now?"

"Because you want a divorce." He spoke softly, leaning in. "Don't you?"

"More than anything." Annie smiled.

Renee returned with a bottle of champagne and two

crystal flutes. She filled the glasses, leaving the bottle chilling in a bucket beside the table.

Nate raised his glass, holding it out until Annie reluctantly did the same. "To our marriage," he said, clinking the crystal against hers.

"And its timely dissolution," Annie mumbled, quickly bringing the glass to her lips. The golden, bubbly liquid filled her mouth, the flavor surprisingly pleasant and sweet on her tongue. It splashed into her empty stomach, creating a warming sensation that started spreading throughout her body. "Mmm…" She sighed, taking another sip.

Nate watched her suspiciously with his full flute held in midair as she drained half her glass and set it down. "Do you like it?"

"I do." Annie smiled again, the expression coming much easier than it had before. She had been wound so tightly today, but in an instant she was starting to feel languid, like a house cat stretched out in a sunbeam.

Renee returned just then, ready to take their orders. Annie was suddenly ravenously hungry, ordering more than she would normally. Nate actually smirked through a sip of champagne as she ordered the bacon-wrapped filet and shrimp with the garlic mashed potatoes. He didn't even know she intended to have dessert, as well. The crème brûlée at Carolina's was not to be missed.

Renee finished writing and took their menus before she offered to refill her empty glass. Annie accepted gratefully. "What kind of champagne is this? It tastes better than I expected it to."

"French. And expensive." Nate frowned, as though he were pinching pennies. More likely he was irritated that his power play hadn't turned out as he'd hoped.

"Good." She nearly giggled as she sipped the golden

bubbles. The champagne had immediately gone to Annie's head. She'd told Nate once that she didn't drink because she didn't like losing control. That was true, but
not entirely. The other reason was that she was a light-
weight. Add in that she hadn't eaten since her layover in
Dallas, and you had a recipe for disaster.

She considered tearing off a hunk of the warm bread to
soak up some of the alcohol, but resisted. For one thing,
she didn't need the extra carbs. Two, she wanted to be
drunk. If he insisted she drink, he was going to find out
how big a mistake that truly was.

They sat silently for a few minutes after that. Annie
ate her salad ferociously, stopping only long enough to
drain her second glass of champagne and pour a third.

Annie knew she should stop, but she just didn't want
to. She didn't want to sit here, pretending to be in love
with him. She couldn't play nice while her heart was aching every time he looked at her. It was too painful. She
wasn't happy about the way things had ended between
them, but she couldn't change it. There was a good reason she'd run and stayed gone for so many years.

And yet she had a responsibility to fulfill, so she
slipped off her heel and let her bare foot roam up under
the cuff of his pant leg.

Nate jumped in his seat, his knees whacking the bottom of the table and jingling the glassware. Several
people turned to look in their direction, but he quickly
recovered with a nervous straightening of his tie.

Annie ignored his pointed gaze, tipping a sip of champagne into her mouth. "You said we had to be convincing, darling." She set the flute back onto the table with
a sweet smile and stroked the firm muscles of his calves
with her toes. "Besides, we both know I lose all my good
sense when I'm around you."

* * *

Nate looked at the woman who had occupied his thoughts for the past three years. The giggling mess across the table was not exactly as he remembered her. She'd managed to eat every morsel laid in front of her and drink at least four flutes of champagne.

At the moment she was licking the spoon after her last bite of crème brûlée as though she might never eat again.

He had to give her credit, though. She'd kept up her end of the bargain. Through the meal, she'd looked at him adoringly, fed him bites of her food and leaned in to kiss him on more than one occasion. Anyone watching their exchange would think they were blissfully in love.

The truth was that she was blissfully drunk. A quick glance under the table revealed his biggest fear— four-inch stilettos. Did the woman not own any sensible shoes? There was no way she would be able to walk out of this restaurant with any dignity at all.

Nate quickly surveyed the room. Their dinner had run quite late and most people had cleared out for the evening. It was a Thursday, a big night at some places in Vegas for senior bingo, but that wasn't the crowd he drew at the Sapphire. If she was determined to embarrass him, she'd chosen the wrong day.

He quickly scribbled his information onto the restaurant tab, tipping Renee heavily. Then he turned back to Annie with a heavy sigh. "Are you finished?"

She reluctantly put her spoon back into the empty ramekin. "I guess so. That is, if I can manage to stand up."

Nate moved quickly, coming around to help her. She stood, probably too fast, and wobbled for a second before gripping his outstretched arm for dear life.

"Why don't you—?"

"No," she insisted, her brow drawn in drunken concentration. "I can *do* this." She took a few unsteady steps beside him and then seemed to recover nicely. Just as they approached the entrance to the restaurant, her heel turned beneath her and she threw herself onto the maître d' stand.

"Whoa there," she said with an uncertain laugh. In one quick motion, she righted herself and plucked off her shoes. "Much better," she said, wiggling her toes into the plush and wildly colored casino carpeting.

"What are you doing? You can't just walk through here barefoot." Nate frowned.

Annie laughed, walking on and answering casually over her shoulder. "I know the owner. He won't mind."

Nate was quick to follow. "I mean it isn't safe. You could step on something. Drunks break glasses in here all the time. We try to get it all up, but you never know. Besides, the floor could be filthy."

"You are an old ninny, Nathan." Annie turned to him and planted her hands on her hips. Her heels dangled helplessly at her side as she wrinkled her nose and actually stuck out her tongue at him.

He could barely trust his eyes. No one on the poker circuit would believe this story if he told it later. *The Barracuda,* drunk and acting like a fool, albeit a beautiful one. It was unheard of. Unprecedented. And hysterical.

The bubble of laughter rose up in his throat. He couldn't contain it. The pent-up frustration and disappointment and confusion of the last three years all pooled together at once and exploded out of him in a roar of laughter. His whole body shook with the power of it. Nate actually bowed over, his hands braced on his knees as he chuckled until tears started gathering in the corners of his eyes.

He looked up to see the laughter had doubled Annie's

irritation. Her expression only made it harder for him to breathe. Nate stood up, attempting to calm himself and wiping his face with the back of his hand. It was incredibly therapeutic—more so than the glasses of scotch or hours angrily lifting weights in the hotel gym.

"That's it, I'm leaving!" she announced, turning and marching away from the restricted area, shoes in hand.

"Annie, come back here." Nate jogged after her, reaching out to grasp her wrist and jerk her to a stop.

"Let go of me," she whined, her anger doused by the champagne and reducing her to childish behavior.

Nate tightened his grip. "I will not. You're going the wrong way. The elevator upstairs is over there." He pointed.

Annie looked around her, confused, and then recognized her mistake. She started walking in the correct direction but was once again tugged to a stop by Nate. "Would you *please* let go of me?" she asked, exasperated.

Nate shook his head. "Not until you put your shoes back on."

"Are you going to make me?" Annie taunted, tugging away again.

That was the wrong thing to say. Nate couldn't take any more of this. If she wanted to make a scene in his casino, so be it, but he wouldn't be the one everyone whispered about tomorrow. In one quick motion, he bent and scooped Annie up, tossing her over his shoulder like a kicking, screaming sack of potatoes.

"What the…?" she cried in surprise, but it was already too late.

Nate marched through the casino, his arms tightly gripping her legs to his chest to keep her from kicking him. Her free fists were already pounding at his back, but that was easy to ignore.

"Put me down, Nathan Reed! Put me down this instant," Annie wailed.

Nate chuckled and disregarded her, walking through the casino as though it were his dry cleaning over his shoulder instead of his wife. Eyes were glued to him from every side, but he didn't care. He nodded politely to the staff as he passed, just as he did every day.

"Nathan!" she howled.

"You're only drawing more attention to yourself by yelling, Annie."

The squirming mass on his shoulder quieted at once, although she still attempted a kick every few feet for good measure. Nate looked up at one of the domed ceiling cameras. He had no doubt that Gabe was watching them and laughing hysterically in the security office. He'd have to remember to save this tape for posterity. Or future blackmail.

Nate swiped his badge and ducked through the doorway to the restricted area. Once safely enclosed, Annie began kicking and screaming anew.

"Put me down!"

"Nope." Nate called his private elevator and ignored the stiletto heels being pummeled against him. Instead, he held her legs more tightly. He enjoyed the feel of her in his arms, even in the less than ideal circumstance. The warm scent of her perfume was instantly familiar, stirring a heat in his veins. He couldn't resist letting his fingertips softly stroke the smooth skin of her legs. Her skirt was long enough to protect her virtue as he'd walked through the casino, but it still provided him an excellent view of the firm thighs he'd missed all these years.

When the doors opened, he stepped inside the elevator. Now that they were out of the public view, he could put her down, even though he didn't want to. Nate wrapped one arm behind her legs and another across the small of her back, slowly easing her to the floor. She clung to him, their bodies in full contact as she slid, inch by inch, to the ground. The simple motion caused a delicious friction as he felt her every curve press into him.

When her feet finally touched the ground, Annie looked up at him, her eyes blazing with blue fire. But not from desire. The impact of the powerful moment was overshadowed by his stunt. Either that or it just made her angrier that she reacted to him.

"You jackass," she screeched as she swung her purse to strike him. Nate reached out and grabbed hold of her wrist before she could make contact. It only fueled her irritation. "How dare you manhandle me like that? I...I am not one of your employees you can shuffle around at will! I—"

Nate interrupted her tirade by capturing her mouth with his. He wasn't about to let her poisonous words ruin this moment. Annie fought it for only a moment before succumbing to her desires and wrapping her arms around his neck to tug him closer. The kiss was hard and almost desperate as they came together for their first real kiss in three years.

He backed her up until she was pinned against the brass doors of the elevator. With the heavy thud of their bodies against the cold metal, it was as though the floodgates had opened. Nate could feel the intensity of their touches start to build, their hands feverishly dancing over their bodies as their mouths threatened to devour each other. He'd waited three long years to touch her body again and at last, he could.

His palm cupped her breast through the silky fabric of her shirt. She moaned, her body arching to press against him. "Oh, Nate," she whispered.

The elevator came to a stop. Nate pulled her to him as the doors slid open behind her. He knew that he should let her go. This was not part of his plan, but he just couldn't make himself do it. It felt right to have Annie in his arms again, even if she'd done nothing but aggravate him all evening.

He let his thumb gently trace the line of her jaw and relished the feel of her soft skin. Her eyes closed and lips parted slightly with a soft intake of breath. Her whole body relaxed into him, her anger a distant memory.

Annie opened her eyes and looked up at him. There was an obvious invitation in her blue gaze. Despite her earlier protests, too much champagne and not enough kissing had changed her mind. It had changed his, too. No matter what happened after they married, the times they'd spent in one another's arms had always been fantastic. Every nerve in his body urged him to indulge it. If he stepped off this elevator with her, he would have her naked and in his bed in minutes. Exactly what he'd told Gabe he wouldn't do.

So what the hell was he doing?

Nate straightened up and gently grasped Annie's shoulders. "Good night, Annie."

She frowned for a moment before he gave her a firm but gentle push. The movement was enough to send her stumbling backward out of the elevator and into the foyer of his suite. He quickly hit the button, closing the doors and sending him back to the casino, leaving them both aroused and alone.

Four

Annie was awakened the next morning by the sound of the shower running. She pushed herself up in bed, eyeing the pristine blankets on Nate's side. He must have slept on the couch.

She hoped he had a crick in his neck from it. After he'd wound her up then dropped her like a rock last night, he deserved it. When he'd kissed her so fiercely, she'd thought that perhaps he was as attracted to her as she still was to him. But when she stumbled back onto the landing and watched the cold, impassive expression on his face as the elevator doors closed, she'd known she was wrong.

Nate hated her. Anything and everything he could do to make her miserable—including turning her on and leaving her unsatisfied—was on the table for the next week. He'd lured her back to Las Vegas with this poker tournament just so he could slowly torture her. It was a devious plot, and a part of her knew she deserved it for leaving the way she had, but that didn't mean she was just going to sit back and take it.

If Nate thought he could use their physical connection to manipulate her, he had another think coming. Two could play at that game. He'd desired her once; she could make him want her again. Silently seducing and manipulating men was at least half of her poker strategy. That's why her sweaters were so low cut and her skirts were so tight. Poker required concentration, and she'd learned early on that being attractive was one of her biggest advantages in a game dominated by men.

The water turned off and Annie heard the glass door of the shower stall open and close. She quickly smoothed her hands over her hair and wished she was wearing pajamas with more seductive appeal. Her thin cotton shorts didn't quite fit the bill, so she tugged up the sheets so only her skimpy matching tank top would show.

The door opened a moment later to reveal a wet and steamy Nate. He had a dark blue towel wrapped low on his hips that drew the eye down his hard belly to the line of darkening hair that disappeared beneath the terry cloth. His golden curls were damp, his face freshly shaved. Annie tried to focus on looking alluring, but it was hard when she was face-to-face with a body like his. Every inch was hard-carved muscle.

Nate paused in the doorway. His glance flicked briefly to the snug fit of her top over her breasts and returned to her eyes. "Good, you're up. You need to get ready. Gabe will be here in about an hour to brief you on our strategy."

Annie abandoned her attempt at alluring Nate and frowned. "Strategy?"

"For you snitching, as you've called it."

Annie had been so distracted by last night's events that she'd forgotten about the deal she'd made. She wasn't just posing as his happy bride in public and feuding with him in private. She was supposed to be spying. Cracking the ring. Earning her freedom. The tournament officially started tomorrow, but everyone would be arriving today for the kickoff, registration and the cocktail party.

"Okay." She sighed. "As long as you promise to keep Gabe on his leash. Putting up with his crap was not part of the agreement."

Nate nodded and disappeared into the closet. "I'll do my best." He came back out with a blue pin-striped shirt and a navy suit. He laid them across his side of the bed and went back toward the bathroom. The towel fell away as he tugged on it, giving her a glimpse of his tight, bare rear end as he disappeared out of sight.

Annie immediately averted her eyes and took a deep breath, wishing away the warm stirring of desire in her belly. Her attraction to Nate was counterproductive. She needed to get her body and brain on the same page, and fast. She flung back the sheets and slipped quietly from the bedroom. If he was going to parade around naked while he got ready, it was probably a good idea for her to go get some coffee in the kitchen.

She was sitting at the granite-topped breakfast bar, taking her first tentative sips of the hot drink, when Nate strode into the kitchen, fully dressed and handsome as ever. He poured his own mug and turned to face her.

"What do you have on your agenda today?"

Annie frowned. She didn't like having to report her every move. She didn't have any firm plans, but she didn't care for him knowing each step of her day, either. He'd been that way after they got married. He didn't have the ability to be with her every moment while he ran the casino, but he checked in with her enough to make her thankful she had an unlimited texting plan. "I don't know yet. Is there something we have to do?"

"I don't think so. After we meet with Gabe, you'll probably have most of the afternoon free until the cocktail party. Do you have a dress for tonight?"

Annie arched her eyebrow at him over her mug. Yes,

she had a dress. She had two, in fact. She'd been planning to wear the more elegant and tasteful of the two dresses, but as punishment for his behavior last night, she was going to wear the sexier, more scandalous one. If she was successful, tonight *he* would be the one tossing and turning with unfulfilled fantasies. "Yes," was all she replied.

"Good. Most of the players start arriving today and will be registering. Perhaps this afternoon you can make some headway in your investigation by socializing with them."

Annie hated the idea of turning her social time with friends into a manhunt. "My sister comes in today. I'll probably have dinner with her and meet you at the party."

"I forgot you have a sister. What's her name again?"

"Tessa. She's playing in the tournament, too."

"Good. I'll be happy to finally meet her."

Annie swallowed a large gulp of coffee and tried not to choke on it. "Yeah, I'm going to have to talk to her before we play happy family and do formal introductions."

"You're not telling her what we're really doing, are you?"

Annie shook her head. "No, but the cover story will raise enough questions. Commitmentphobia runs in our bloodline, and she's even more firmly entrenched in our family traditions than I am."

"She disapproves of us?"

"Tessa certainly did the first time, especially after I left and she got to rub it in my face. I have no doubt she'll give me hell for getting mixed up with you twice."

"What did your mother think about us?"

"I come from a long line of independent, distrustful women," she explained.

"Ahh…" Nate said. "Our marriage was not their favorite dinnertime subject."

"I don't suppose so. We're really not that close. I haven't seen my mother in several years. She's in Brazil at the moment. She was in Portugal before that." Annie at least tried to travel with a purpose and had found a career to soothe the itch to move. She had a condo in Miami as her home base between tournaments. Her mother just wandered to wherever the wind blew her. Annie had seen her four times in the ten years since she'd moved out on her own. "Are you close with your family?"

"Define close." He laughed. "It depends. I've always been pretty close with my father and my grandfather before he died. Dad got a wild haircut and bought a ranch in Texas a few years ago, but until then, almost my whole family lived here in Vegas. The Reeds have been here since 1964, when my grandfather decided to relocate from Los Angeles and open a hotel."

Annie knew her mother couldn't even tell her where she *was* in 1964, much less every place she'd been since then. "A family legacy, then."

"Yes." He straightened up, a smile of pride curling his lips. "I was happy to be able to make the Sapphire everything it could be. I pretty much grew up running the halls and doing my homework in my father's office. When the hotel was passed on to me, I knew it was important to keep my grandfather's dream alive."

"What about your mother?"

The light of pride in Nate's eyes dimmed, his smile fading just slightly enough for her to notice. "I haven't seen my mother since I was twelve." His words were cold and matter-of-fact. "She got tired of the casino life and took off one night."

Annie felt a sharp pang of guilt stab her in the gut like a knife. He spoke impassively on the topic, but she could tell it was a sore subject, having happened to him so young. No wonder he seemed to be so focused on punishing Annie for abandoning their marriage. She'd not only left him, but she'd jabbed him in his most tender spot. Hit his Achilles without aiming.

She swallowed hard and shifted her guilty gaze down into her coffee cup. "I didn't know that." Would it have kept her from leaving? Probably not. But she might have handled it differently if she'd known about his mother. That was just one more reason why marrying a stranger was so treacherous. You had no idea how badly you could really hurt someone and not even know it.

"How could you know? I don't talk about it."

"I know, but…" she began, but couldn't think of what else to say other than the most overdue words of all. "I'm sorry I left like she did. It was cowardly of me not to talk to you about the anxiety I was having. If I had known about your mother, I—"

"Don't," Nate interrupted, his jaw tight. "Don't handle me with kid gloves like I'm damaged somehow, because I'm not. You didn't hurt me, Annie. I wouldn't let you."

He turned his back to her and put his empty mug in the sink. Glancing quickly at his watch, he said, "Go get dressed. Gabe will be here soon."

Nate was already in a bad mood, brought on by an uncomfortable night's rest and the miserable and near-constant ache in his groin from being so near to Annie. Talking about his mother had been the damned cherry on his day so far. But even then, he couldn't help but be amused by the animosity between Gabe and Annie. They were glaring at each other across the table as though *they* were the feuding couple. They'd been silent and still for the past few minutes as Nate gathered paperwork from his desk and brought it over to the conference table.

"We're on the same team," he reminded them.

His words did little to unwind the tension in Gabe's shoulders. He was suspicious of Annie, and nothing Nate said or did was going to change it. Gabe was good at reading people. Nate tried not to ask him too much about the things he'd done when serving in the military, but he knew Gabe's instincts were always spot-on. He hoped his friend's suspicion of Annie was just residual distrust from years ago, but there was no way to know for certain. Annie was a stranger. His wife...his past lover... but still a stranger.

Gabe opened his portfolio and focused on the task at hand. "I've done quite a bit of recon. Talked to a few of my sources. Here's a short list of our most likely candidates." He slid the paper with ten or twelve names on it across the table to Annie. "These might be your best bets to start with."

Nate watched Annie review the names, her face betraying none of her opinions. She had one of the best poker faces in the game. "If I had to put my money on one of them," he said, "I'd bet on Eddie Walker. He reeks of it, but he's slippery."

Annie nodded but again didn't offer any information she might have on him. Nate was certain she'd heard something about Walker over the years. He was practically notorious for never getting caught red-handed. It had always confused Nate because, to be honest, he didn't seem that bright. But apparently he had a mind for dirty dealing. Or he had a silent partner who was the real brains behind the operation.

"You can go ahead and cross off Mike Stewart," she said, her face still blank, as though they were perched in front of playing cards instead of paperwork. "And Bob Cooke."

"How can you be so sure?" Gabe challenged.

Annie shot a lethal gaze at his head of security. "You brought me into this because I have inside knowledge of these people," she said sharply. "If you contradict everything I tell you, this whole ruse is pointless. I'm telling you they're not cheats."

"*I* didn't bring you into this, Nate did. Personally, I don't think we can trust you. You say they're on the level, but we've got no way of knowing you aren't just protecting your friends. Or cohorts," he added with an accusatory tone.

Annie sighed and shook her head. "Neither are friends. Or cohorts, *thankyouverymuch.* Here's some honest inside information for you. Mike is actually a pervert who cheats on his wife. He comes on to me at every tournament, even when she's with him. But he's not a poker cheat. And neither is Bob. Bob is bipolar. His playing fluctuates wildly depending on whether or not he's taken his medication. Recheck your sources," she said, shoving the paper back at Gabe.

"What about Jason Devries?"

"Jason won the tournament two years ago and typically makes it to the final table."

"So?" Gabe challenged.

"So," Annie continued, "he doesn't need the help. You're looking for someone who improves suddenly or performs well inconsistently. If they're smart, the people behind this will rarely take the grand prize. It's too obvious. You're looking for a lower-level player. Someone who will slink away with their eighth-place prize money and never rouse suspicion. These people aren't stupid or someone would've caught them by now."

Nate's eyebrows went up at Annie's bold words. Perhaps she wouldn't hold back as much as they thought.

Gabe didn't appear as impressed. "I want you to wear a wire."

Even Nate was surprised at Gabe's sudden declaration. They'd never discussed that possibility before. If they had, he would've eased her into the idea instead of bulldozing her like that. His friend knew how to handle suspects and terrorists but not a woman like Annie.

"Absolutely not." Annie crossed her arms over her chest, her brow knitting together in a defiant frown. A bit of her facade crumbled at the challenge, and Nate noticed a very becoming blush rising to her cheeks. All the times they argued, he was too busy being upset to really appreciate how beautiful she was when she let emotion slip through. Annie was far more attractive than the Barracuda.

"I don't trust her," Gabe said, not caring that Annie was three feet away. Nate reluctantly returned to the conversation, taking in Gabe's rapid explanation. "You think this is the only way, but I disagree. If you insist on involving her, the only way we can be certain, that we can know for sure she's doing her part and not tipping anyone off, is if she wears a wire."

"I'm not doing it. This was not part of the agreement."

Nate held his hands up. "Let's just talk about this for a second, please. Annie, I know you don't like the idea of it, but wearing a wire may actually be a good idea. For reasons *other*," he emphasized, "than the ones Gabe suggested. It would take the pressure off you to remember everything people tell you. Someone on the listening end could be taking notes and doing investigations on players while you're still sitting at the table. Gabe could start pulling security tapes and adding plainclothes guards to keep watch."

"Some of these people could be dangerous. Suspecting

me of spying is one thing, but catching me with a wire? You don't know what they're capable of."

"You would be surrounded by security at all times. There's no way you could be any safer. The audio recordings are the evidence we need to convict someone. With security cameras the way they are, it's very hard to capture someone cheating when they're a professional. The tapes could make all the difference." He urged her to consider it. He didn't want to start bullying her around and force her to do it by holding the divorce over her head again. She'd completely shut down and that wouldn't get them anywhere.

"I can guarantee your safety. I wouldn't let anyone hurt you, Annie. I promise you that."

Annie looked up, her concerned gaze meeting his serious one. He meant every word. Nate might want to punish his wife for what she'd done, but if anyone else touched a hair on her head, they'd regret it.

It seemed to calm her. After a moment she nodded softly and looked away. "Fine," she said, clearly defeated and unhappy about it. "But—" she pointed sharply at Gabe "—he doesn't get to tape it under my blouse."

"Fair enough," Nate said. "Gabe, why don't you go get the equipment and we'll do a test run this afternoon before the tournament starts. I want all the bugs worked out so it doesn't interfere with her game."

Gabe nodded and left the room.

"I'm surprised you're so interested in not impacting my card playing. You never seemed to care much for my career before."

Nate knew he hadn't been supportive enough of Annie. For some reason, he hadn't seen playing cards as a career. It was a game, not a job. Time had given him perspective on his mistake, but their disagreement on that point had likely been a deal breaker for her. He didn't push all the blame for their ruined marriage on Annie—just the fact that she'd run instead of talking through their issues like adults.

"I know it's important to you," he said. "But it's also important to us. We need you to play in the tournament as long as possible. If you get eliminated on the first day, we've lost our insider."

Annie glanced down at the table with a sigh. "I should've known you had an angle."

"You're kidding me, right?" Tessa Baracas glared at Annie across the bright turquoise table of the Desert Sapphire's Mexican cantina, Rosa's.

Annie didn't look at her. Instead, she focused her gaze on her uneaten dinner and the platinum wedding band searing her finger. She hadn't been looking forward to having this conversation, especially with a wire taping their every word. "No, I'm serious."

"Did you not learn your lesson the last time?" Tessa looked horrified. Her skin, so pale compared to Annie's olive tone, was even lighter with shock, if that was possible. Her red-gold hair was pulled back into a tight, sleek ponytail, her jewel-blue eyes wide with surprise and confusion.

The eyes were the sole feature Annie and Tessa seemed to share. The sparkling-blue color was the most noticeable trait they'd inherited from their mother. Sure, they had similar builds, with ample curves and heart-shaped faces, but that's where the similarities ended.

They had different fathers, ones that their mother had apparently hand selected for the sole purpose of creating beautiful babies. Tessa's father was a ghostly pale Irishman with hair like fire. Annie's father was Italian with jet-black hair, warm brown skin and a full sensual mouth—at least, that was what she'd been told. She'd never met him. Their mother had never stayed in one place long. Never kept a man longer than he was of use to her. Which was why Tessa looked as if Annie had just slapped her across the face when she mentioned reconciling with her husband.

Tessa shook her head and slumped back into her seat. "You need to be focused on the game. Not on men. You of all people should know that. It was the first thing you taught me when I started playing."

"Do you think I planned this? Because I didn't."

Tessa anxiously moved food across her plate with her fork. "You shouldn't have come back here. I just knew you weren't strong enough to resist Nate's magic penis."

A nervous laugh burst from Annie's lips before she could stop it. Her sister's irritated expression immediately silenced it. Tessa was being totally serious. "Did you really just say that?"

"Yes. And it's true."

"Well, first," Annie began, hoping Gabe wasn't listening in yet, "thank you for thinking so little of me that I could be easily manipulated by good sex. Second, a magic pe— *Hell,* I can't even say that, it's so ridiculous. There's no such thing, not even on Nate, as gifted as he might be."

"I just don't trust him. I don't like him."

Annie felt the unfamiliar urge to defend her husband. "You've never even met him," she argued, realizing as she spoke that she'd thought of Nate as her husband for the first time. "You're letting Mom's paranoia cloud your judgment."

"And you're letting the magic penis cloud yours."

Annie sighed. "Please stop calling it that."

"Then is it about the money? I mean, you eloped, so there wasn't a prenup, right?"

Annie's mouth fell open in silent shock for a moment before she could gather the words to respond. Money had never even been a consideration in their relationship. She made great money at poker. She didn't need Nate's fortune, or anyone else's, for that matter. "This doesn't have a thing to do with money, Tessa. How could you even ask me something like that?"

"Okay, if you say so."

Annie tried not to frown at her sister and diverted her angry gaze back at her food. Tessa was so bad at reading people. She was passable at hiding her own emotions but clueless when it came to figuring out her opponents. Until she had that down, she wouldn't go very far in poker.

"Are you finished eating?"

Annie looked down, completely disinterested in her food. "Yeah."

Tessa glanced at the expensive-looking new watch on her wrist. "It's still pretty early. I don't have any plans between now and the cocktail thing tonight. What do you say we hit the tables and play a few hands? I think that would be fun. I haven't gotten to actually play with you in almost forever."

Annie reached for her purse, nodding absently into it. She'd forgotten about the cocktail party, worrying about everything else. Tonight would prove interesting, she had no doubt. Every eye in the room would be on her and her royal-blue dress.

Including Nate's.

Five

"Her sister sucks."

Nate winced at Gabe's sudden observation as they watched Annie and Tessa play from the security room. He'd noticed that, too. He didn't know much about Tessa, but he'd thought the Barracuda's younger sister would be a better player. Had Annie taught her anything about poker, or was she just throwing away her tournament registration fees? Maybe she was having an off night. A very off night. She hadn't won a single hand yet. Another round and she'd be out of chips.

"On a good day, I think Annie could make the Captain look like a novice." Nate spoke the words with a touch of pride. He could appreciate the skill it took for Annie to get this far in her career. Few women did in a field dominated by men like the Captain.

He was famous around the poker circuit for his faded white officer's cap and tacky Hawaiian shirts. He wanted everyone to believe he was some retired Navy officer, but he'd once secretly admitted to Nate's grandfather that he'd bought the hat in a thrift store in 1979.

The Captain was eccentric and annoying as hell to play against, but very, very good. Over the past thirty years, he'd won four championship bracelets, almost always making it to the final table in the main events. He was known for talking his opponents to death. He rambled on with old tales about his so-called Navy days, making crude comments about where he docked his ship in a storm and pestering people with inane nautical trivia.

His plan worked like a charm. His fellow players' concentration crumbled when they went up against the Captain. It was just like when men found themselves face-to-face with *the Barracuda,* although for very different reasons. With Annie, a man's pulse quickened, his groin stirred and he came close to forgetting how to play poker at all.

Nate could understand that. She was a hard woman to resist. Honestly, he wasn't sure how he'd managed to go this long with nothing more than a kiss. This week might be torture for them both.

He swallowed the lump in his throat and shifted in his seat to disguise the uncomfortable development the mere thought of her had brought on. He wasn't sure how much more he could take of looking but not touching. His ability to feign indifference to Annie's allure was eroding away.

He wanted her. Badly. He didn't want to stay married to her or play house with her. He didn't want to have feelings for her. He just needed to touch her and soothe the raging beast inside of him. Perhaps a little indulgence wasn't as dangerous as Gabe seemed to think. It was just sex. The last time they were together the sex was incredible, tainted only by their marriage. Why couldn't they have that physical connection again before they went their separate ways? Certainly he could have sex with Annie and not completely lose his perspective.

Tonight was the tournament kickoff, with a cocktail

reception for the competitors. Nate wanted the Sapphire to put a little old-school Vegas class into it, the way his grandfather would've done it. Tonight there would be flowing drinks, low lighting and sultry music to set the tone for the week.

Of course, having Annie on his arm made it that much more interesting. The thought of her in some slinky dress that clung to each voluptuous curve…the music of her laughter as she sipped a drink… Maybe he would be able to slip an arm around her waist and take her for a spin around the dance floor. Then he could press himself against her stomach and dip down to leave a searing kiss on the soft curve of her neck.

Nate swallowed a groan, shifting in his chair and returning his attention to the monitors. That line of thought really wasn't helping at all.

He narrowed his eyes and shook his head. Tessa really was a horrible player. Her instincts were all off. He could tell that Annie knew it, too. She wasn't going in for the kill. Wasn't trying to lure her sister to bet more when she should.

"Annie looks really uncomfortable," he noted. She always seemed so at ease in her skin, but not tonight. The changes were subtle—she was a blank canvas while she played—but Nate could tell the difference. She fidgeted on her stool; her shoulders were curved over her cards, her muscles tensed. Her gaze darted back and forth around the table, watching the other players.

"Maybe she's nervous about spying for us. It might be too much pressure for her. What if—" A loud hiss of static interrupted Gabe. He frowned, looking down at the control panel and hitting a few buttons without improvement.

"What's wrong?"

"Something's wrong with the wire. We've lost the feed. It must have gotten disconnected."

Nate was glad they were doing this today and not in the middle of tournament play. "I'll go pull her aside and adjust it."

By the time he reached the poker table, Tessa was out. She hovered beside Annie, watching her play with intense study.

Nate had watched them on the black-and-white monitors but hadn't fully appreciated the differences between the sisters until he saw them in person.

They were like night and day. Annie was dark and exotic, Tessa, pale and delicate. They had the same lush curves and straight, shiny hair, but they obviously had different fathers.

Annie had never mentioned a stepfather. Come to think of it, she hadn't mentioned a father at all. Or any family aside from her sister and mother. Of course, this morning she'd practically had to drag information about his family out of him. He normally didn't talk about his mother. Some details of life were better left out of the conversation.

He took a few steps until he was almost touching Annie. Tessa turned briefly, looking him over with the same deep blue gaze as her sister, but didn't acknowledge him aside from the quick, appraising glance. Her disgust was poorly hidden as she turned back, disinterested, to watch Annie play.

It was unnerving to see such animosity coming from eyes so like Annie's. Nate hadn't really anticipated that kind of hostility from her family. What could she have told Tessa about him? He didn't bother to ask; instead, he leaned in to press his chest against the back of Annie's stool.

She stiffened at his touch for a moment before realizing who was behind her and why. "I was wondering where you'd gotten off to. Working, no doubt?" She didn't turn but leaned back ever so slightly against him.

The scent of her shampoo and spicy perfume mingled to tickle his nose. The heat of her body penetrated his suit and almost made him forget why he'd come down here. "Apparently, I'm the only thing around here that works," he hinted. "When you finish this hand, we need a private moment." He leaned in close to her ear so Tessa couldn't hear. "For adjustments."

Annie nodded softly and waited for her turn, tossing a few chips into the pot and causing an older gentleman across from her to shift nervously in his seat. He folded. Another man beside Annie groaned as the river card was laid out. He obviously hadn't mastered his bluff. Annie didn't react at all.

Tessa stood silently, watching, attempting to somehow absorb her sister's skill through sheer concentration. She still didn't look at Nate but for the occasional sideways glance.

He leaned in, pressing his warm lips to the sensitive hollow under Annie's ear. He left a soft kiss that sent a shudder through her body before whispering, "Are you going to introduce me to your sister?"

At that, he could feel Annie's muscles tense under his hands. She hesitated, trying to focus on the game for a few seconds more. The other player folded at last, allowing her to claim the pot and shift her attention. She turned on her stool to face them.

"Nate, this is my baby sister, Tessa. Tessa, this is…" She paused, struggling to form the words on her lips. "My husband, Nate."

He extended a hand and Tessa warily accepted it. "A pleasure to finally meet some of Annie's family."

Tessa nodded, her expression smug for some reason. "Well, don't hold your breath to meet Mom anytime soon. I may be the only family you ever get to see before *this* is done."

"Well," Annie interjected, sliding from her bar stool, "I'll see you at the party, Tessa. Nate and I have to tend to something."

"Okay. I'd better get upstairs and get ready for tonight."

Annie waved off her sister without a second glance. "Sorry," she muttered once Tessa was gone. She gathered up her winnings slip to take to the cage. "She thought I lost my mind the first time. The idea of us getting back together now is pure insanity to her."

"I'm not worried about what she thinks. But let's go somewhere private."

"Back to the room?"

"No, I need to do a couple things down here before I go upstairs and shower." Nate took her hand and pulled her into an empty corridor that connected the pool area to an older section of the casino. This part of the hotel didn't get as much foot traffic, especially when it was filled with poker players who were generally disinterested in the hotel amenities.

He backed Annie against the wall and stood close to block her from view. His hand went to her back, checking the battery pack. The red light was on, the cord connected. "It must be the microphone," he said.

Annie's eyes widened slightly. "That's, um…between my breasts."

"Maybe the underwire in your bra has pinched it." He slipped his hand beneath her sweater, gliding his fingertips over her stomach and up the length of the wire to where it met with the rough lace of her bra. "I'm not sure what this thing is supposed to—"

Nate caught movement out of the corner of his eye. Someone was coming down the hallway. Without hesitating, he leaned in and kissed Annie. He moved his hand from the wire to the round curve of her breast beside it.

Annie gasped at the sudden change but followed along. She wrapped her arms around his neck and tugged him to her. It might be a kiss to cover their tracks, but this was nothing like their kiss outside of Carolina's. She'd caught him off guard last night, but he could still sense her holding back. Now there was only their very public location to restrain them.

Whoever was in the hallway was long gone, but it didn't matter. The kiss grew harder and more desperate the longer it went on. Her teeth nibbled at his bottom lip. His tongue thrust inside her mouth, tasting her. Annie's body molded against his.

Nate groaned. If he wasn't careful, he'd end up taking her on a nearby blackjack table. He forced himself back, breaking the electric connection that held them together.

"Sweet lord," he whispered against her mouth.

"Yeah," Annie agreed. "Do you think we're good now? With the reception?"

The radio at Nate's hip squawked out Gabe's reply. "We're good," he responded. "Not as good as you two are, though."

Annie pulled away, smoothing her green satin top and brushing at the edges of her smeared lipstick with her fingertips. "Since we're done, I'm going to go," she said, walking unsteadily toward the cashier.

Nate took a deep breath and turned to keep from watching her leave. He didn't think he could take the sight of her sauntering away from him in that tight skirt. He might sweep her over his shoulder and carry her through the casino again.

This time to ravish her.

The suite was silent as Annie stepped off the elevator. She'd expected Nate to be there getting ready, but there was no sign of him. It was just as well. She needed to dress, and the fewer…distractions…the better. She'd already killed too much time lingering downstairs.

She'd been afraid to come up too soon. Afraid to walk in on Nate, wet and naked from another shower. Their kiss in the casino had been to cover their activity in the hall, but once he touched her, the world around them could have vanished. It was unerringly clear—their resistance to one another was wearing away quickly. Their magnetic pull was stronger than her fears or his sense of injustice. None of that mattered when he touched her.

He would have her soon. And she would give herself freely. And enthusiastically. But she would draw the line there. She would indulge no thoughts about a future or a real reconciliation. That's where she went wrong the last time.

Annie stepped quickly down the hall to the bedroom. Nate's suit was thrown across a chair in the corner. The bathroom mirror was still foggy. He had been there. Just briefly.

She kicked off her heels and started absentmindedly undressing, pulling together the pieces of her outfit for the evening.

The heels that matched her royal-blue dress rubbed miserably if she didn't wear stockings. She selected a pair of lace-topped thigh highs from the drawer along with panties. She couldn't wear a bra with her dress, so the wire was out tonight. She peeled away the tape and switched off the battery pack before leaving it on the nightstand. From there, she slipped into the low-riding black lace boy shorts that wouldn't show panty lines. She followed them with the silky, sheer stockings.

Annie stood to retrieve her dress from the closet but stopped when she heard a soft groan from behind her.

"Damn."

She spun in her stocking feet to find Nate in the doorway. Annie was topless but didn't even bother covering herself. She wasn't the most modest person in the world. She had as many body issues as any woman, but she didn't waste the energy worrying about them. Besides, he'd already seen it all and touched a lot of it less than an hour ago.

Letting Nate see what she was wearing—or not wearing in this case—under the dress would make him just that much more miserable tonight.

Probably about as miserable as she would be. Nate looked fabulous. He'd upgraded his suit for a tuxedo. Instead of a tie, he wore a collarless ivory shirt with a shiny black button at his throat. He had a matching ivory handkerchief in his lapel pocket. The suit was custom, of that she was certain. He was not average by any means, and the fit was like a glove.

She wanted to press her bare breasts against the cotton of his shirt and knot her fingers into the curls at his neck. Her nipples tightened at the mere thought of scratching against his suit coat. That, however, would sidetrack the entire evening. Nate had to be at the party. He was throwing it.

Feigning disinterest to disguise her growing desire, she turned and walked into the closet. "Ever hear of knocking?" she asked.

"It's my place. I don't have to knock."

Annie knelt to pick up the heels, slipped the dress from the hanger and draped it over her arm. When she returned to the bedroom he was still there, his hands buried in his pockets, his dark gaze silently appreciative of everything he saw.

"Do you like it?" she asked, holding the dress out for him to see. The dress was short, jewel-blue and had a halter collar with tiny silver studs that wrapped around her throat. The reverse was wide open, draping below the small of her back. It was decadent and sexy, a completely unexpected detail, so she didn't share that with him. She'd let that be a surprise.

"Very much." His voice was slightly strained. "It matches your eyes."

Annie draped the dress over the bedspread. She'd thought the same thing when she bought it. "Are you going to watch me dress?"

Nate thought for a moment, his lips puckered in amusement, his eyes still drinking in every inch of her. He let his gaze dart to the curve of her backside peeking out beneath the lacy panties. "No…I just wanted to let you know I was going down to the reception to make sure everything is set up."

Annie nodded. "I'll meet you there in a bit."

Nate eyed his watch. "Shall I order you a drink?"

"A diet soda this time." Annie smiled. "Thank you." The last thing she needed was a repeat of the champagne incident.

Nate returned the smile, clearly following her thoughts. His gaze slowly traveled over her once more, then he turned and disappeared down the hall.

Annie had to take a moment to sit on the edge of the bed. He'd looked at her so intently she could almost feel it like a caress. The heat of it traveled over her body, making her breasts ache and her skin tighten. A deep throb of longing echoed in her core, acknowledging the connection between them that she denied. Perhaps tonight was the night.

A half hour later, she was downstairs and heading toward the Sapphire Lounge. The slinky bar was usually packed with tourists and locals alike for mingling and dancing to the sounds of the talented jazz singer and pianist who played there.

Tonight it was reserved for those registered in the tournament and the bigwigs from the sponsors. A quick look around the room confirmed that many of the players had brought their wives. That would cut down on how many of them would ask her to dance. She was relieved.

It was a male-dominated sport, and wives didn't always follow their men along from game to game. Nate had gone out of his way to schedule several events at this year's tournament to include them. Tonight was the reception, of course, but over the next week there was also a poker widows' luncheon and an excursion to Hoover Dam and the Grand Canyon. Nate was good with the details.

As Annie stepped into the lounge, she was greeted warmly by several friends. Benny the Shark hollered, "The Barracuda!" and before she knew it, the Captain was clasping her in a musty bear hug and Eli was trying to buy her a drink.

She declined, trying to disentangle herself, but got stuck chitchatting. They were boisterous and loud, going on and on as though they hadn't all seen each other in Atlantic City a month ago. The Captain was wearing his best Hawaiian shirt—it was a special occasion, after all—but most of the others had forgone their jeans and polo shirts for suits and ties. It was a nice change. She almost didn't recognize Rodney Chan, he cleaned up so well.

Of course, the first words out of his mouth were about her and Nate. It was apparently all over the tournament that someone had snagged the Barracuda. Most of her friends had already heard the whispers, and those that hadn't turned to her in surprise and pumped her for details. Annie wasn't very close with her family, so these were the people who knew her the best. They were also the people who would be the most surprised to see that ring on her finger.

Annie took the congratulatory drink forced on her by Eli and chatted for a while before she made excuses to leave and find Nate. She weaved through the crowd but couldn't see him anywhere. Normally he stood out, a head taller with a booming voice and contagious laughter, but the lounge was too full tonight to find anyone.

She was about to give up and find a stool at the bar when she caught the flame of red hair out of the corner of her eye.

Tessa was looking lovely in a Kelly-green satin cocktail dress. It was strapless, showcasing her creamy, flawless skin. Her hair was down now, falling over her bare shoulders like liquid fire. Annie had always been jealous of her younger sister's hair. It only got worse as Tessa got older and grew into a stunningly beautiful woman. She was only twenty-two and had a lot of growing up left to do, but she was off to a fine start.

A man with his back to Annie stood near to Tessa, slipping a hand around her waist. It was an intimate gesture, one Annie was not accustomed to when it involved her baby sister.

Then he turned to speak to someone and she saw his face. It was Eddie Walker. A touch of bile started rising in her throat, but she forced it back down. *Hell, no.* That dirty bastard was not touching her sister.

Before she could stop herself, Annie marched across the dance floor and grabbed her sister by the wrist.

"Hey!" Tessa protested as Annie tugged, but she stayed firmly in place with the assistance of Eddie's grip around her waist.

"Tessa, come with me *right now.*" Annie could hear her mother's scolding tone in her voice.

The demand obviously chafed her sister's pride and she clung with more determination to Eddie. "No."

"Don't get your panties in a twist, Annie. This is a party." The leech had the nerve to speak to her, a cocky grin spread across his face. "It might be better if you just stayed out of this."

"Don't you tell me what is or isn't my business when it comes to my sister and a sleaze like you. Tessa, come on." She tugged again, this time shooting eye daggers at Eddie until he released her. She pulled Tessa into a dark corner near the ladies' room, well out of anyone's earshot.

"What is *wrong* with you?" Tessa complained, yanking her hand away.

"Me? What's wrong with *you?* Eddie Walker? Are you kidding me?"

Tessa's face hardened, her jaw setting defiantly as she crossed her arms over her chest. "You're one to talk, *Mrs. Reed.*"

"That's not what I mean. Eddie is…" Annie struggled to find the right words.

"Wonderful?"

"No. He's a dirty, stinking, lying poker cheat."

Tessa's eyes widened for a moment, an expression of shock paralyzing her mouth in an open O. Apparently she thought Eddie's reputation hadn't spread that far. Had he convinced her that no one knew about his activities?

"Please don't get involved with him."

"It's too late, Annie. I've been seeing him for almost six months."

Six months? How had Annie missed this? She wasn't very social with Tessa, but she must've been trying fairly hard to avoid the subject this long. Why did she have to break her relationship streak of two months with a scumbag like Walker? "He's bad news, Tessa."

"Oh, please. You're just jealous."

"Why would I be jealous? He's not a great catch, Tess. You've known him six months. I've known him six *years*. Everyone knows that he plays a dirty game. They just haven't caught him yet."

Tessa's expression changed then. It almost beamed with subdued pride. Was she honestly proud that Eddie was too crafty to be caught? That would all change, and quickly, with Nate involved. He wouldn't tolerate it in his hotel and he was using Annie to ensure it.

"I know what I'm doing."

Annie sighed. There was no more sense in arguing. For one thing, Tessa was stubborn. Telling her she couldn't do something was like a challenge. Annie realized she'd already made that mistake when she saw the defiant look in her sister's eyes. Second, the harder Annie pushed, the more closed off Tessa would become. They weren't close, but the gap could easily widen. She couldn't afford that, especially now.

Her sister was playing with fire, thinking it was safe because she believed she was the one in control. How quickly would she get burned?

Annie knew this was her last chance to say her peace, to warn her sister before Gabe would start listening in on every conversation she had. "Just be careful. Don't get in too deep with him."

Tessa exhaled roughly, nodding slightly in relief that her sister backed off the uncomfortable subject. "I don't get in too deep with men." She smiled. "You should know that. You used to be the same way."

Six

By the time Nate looked down at his watch, the cocktail party had been going strong for over an hour. Certainly Annie was here somewhere. Fashionably late had passed quite a while ago. He'd kept an eye out while glad-handing all of his VIPs, but there'd been no sign of her. At least not from his side of the bar. He'd thought there was no way he'd miss that blue dress, but he'd underestimated how many people would be here tonight.

Then he saw her.

Annie came charging from the bathroom, leaving her befuddled sister in her wake.

Nate's breath caught in his chest at the sight of her. The dress was like a dream, the bright blue playing beautifully against her tan skin and jet-black hair. The high, firm breasts he'd seen earlier moved tantalizingly beneath the fabric as she walked, reminding him that they were free beneath it. The short cut of the dress highlighted the sculpted muscles of her calves and rhinestone-covered sandals.

In that instant, the last of his resistance was blown to pieces. He would have Annie in his bed tonight, consequences be damned. He could no longer convince himself otherwise.

She looked gorgeous…and agitated. Her skin was flushed, her brow furrowed, her delicate jaw tight. That was unusual for her. He didn't like it. Not one bit. It made him wish he could listen in on the sisters' conversation. It was a shame she wasn't wearing the wire tonight, but that dress left no place to hide it. It barely hid what it was supposed to.

Nate signaled for a refill on his vodka tonic and a Diet Coke from the bartender and carried the drinks to where she'd stopped. She was leaning against one of the high-top bar tables, her beautiful face buried in her hands.

"Here's your soda." He leaned over to her. "I can have Mike add a shot of rum if you need it."

Annie stood up with a start, her face quickly composing into her usual cool demeanor. "Oh! You startled me." Whatever was bothering her was rapidly compartmentalized and put away. She eyed the glass in his hand and accepted it with a forced smile. "Thank you. The rum won't be necessary."

Nate came to her side, leaning in to kiss her on the cheek and slip an arm around her waist. To his surprise, his hand came in contact with her bare, smooth skin instead of fabric. Thoughts of her earlier agitation vanished as he let his fingers travel across her skin, searching for where the dress began. He was forced to stop short of public fondling.

"You should've told me," he murmured into her ear over the buzz of the crowd.

A slight look of panic widened her eyes for a moment. "Told you what?"

He let his warm palm press into the small of her back, the heat of her skin almost burning him. "That you could only afford half a dress. I would've bought you a whole one if I'd known."

Annie sighed, wrinkling her nose and sipping her drink. "You don't like it?"

Nate chuckled. "Of course I *like* it. The problem is that so does every other man in this place."

"Ahh." She smiled. "You're jealous."

He had every damn right to be. Everyone knew the Barracuda used her looks to distract her opponents. She'd developed a long list of admirers over the years as a result. The mere thought of another man looking at Annie like that was enough to send his blood pressure skyrocketing. Even after all this time there was a primitive part of Nate that still considered her to be *his*.

"I am not jealous. Simply territorial." He picked up his glass and sipped.

"Are you going to piss on me?"

Nate nearly choked on his vodka tonic. Annie was unpredictable. He had to give her that. "I don't think that will be necessary." He coughed.

"Good. I don't think this fabric is washable." Annie smiled, taking another sip of her drink. The worries of just minutes ago were so far buried Nate wouldn't know they were even there if he hadn't seen her upset.

"Are you having a good time?"

Annie shrugged. "It's a very nice party."

"I think so. But you didn't answer my question."

She turned, her blue eyes penetrating him as she attempted to read what he was really after. "Yes, I am," she said slowly, watching his face for changes.

Nate nodded and took another sip of his drink. "A poker player should be a better liar. What happened with Tessa just now?"

"Nothing." Annie responded too quickly, breaking eye contact and gazing down into her glass.

Nate looked in the direction Annie had come from. Her sister had sat down at a table, but she wasn't alone. Now she was in the arms of a despicable man. If Tessa were his sister, he'd be pretty damn upset, too. "Hanging out with Eddie Walker isn't nothing."

Annie's head snapped up, her eyes narrowing at him. "She just told me they're dating and have been for several months. I had no idea."

Nate raised an eyebrow at her response. Weren't sisters supposed to share everything? "That's no revelation. I can see that much just by the way he touches her."

They both turned to watch Eddie and Tessa in the corner. They were talking to one another in the dark, rounded booth. Their body language screamed sex; their legs crossed together as they leaned in and gazed into one another's eyes. Eddie had one hand on her bare knee, the other rubbing strands of her red hair together between his fingertips.

Nate turned to watch Annie instead of the secluded lovebirds. Her nose was wrinkled, her brow furrowed again in concern. Whether or not she had prior knowledge, she obviously didn't care for this love match. Eddie had a rotten reputation, and he wasn't the kind of guy you'd pick for your sister.

Eddie had been his number-one candidate to watch from the beginning. Everyone knew he was cheating; they just couldn't catch him. Whether he was involved in the big operation the tournament sponsors were after, he wasn't certain.

That's why he'd asked Annie to help him. She could lure him out, get evidence to charge him. It required someone on the inside who really knew the game. Annie was perfect for the job. She wouldn't let anyone get in the way of her winning the grand prize, and he had no doubt she would do what she could to stop Eddie. And now that her sister was dating him, what better way to break them up than to send the creep to jail?

He would talk to Annie about that. But not tonight.

Tonight he had better things on his mind. Like getting Annie back in his bed. He'd fought with himself since the moment she'd arrived, but damned if he didn't still want her. Even after everything. Their three years apart had only amplified the hum of arousal that buzzed through his veins. He wouldn't love Annie. He wouldn't even let himself care about her. But he could get his fill of her before she walked away.

When Nate was a child, his grandfather had once given him a huge bag of cherry jelly beans. With his father busy and his mother off shopping, he'd sat in front of the television one afternoon and eaten the whole bag. Nate had never been so sick in his life. To this day, he couldn't abide cherry jelly beans. Or cherry anything, for that matter.

Perhaps the same would be true of Annie. Resisting was the wrong tactic. He needed to fully indulge himself in her soft body and silky skin. Overdose on her. Get her out of his system. And maybe by week's end, when the divorce paperwork was drawn up, he would be just as disinterested by the thought of her as he was by that noxious candy.

Nate eyed a tray of appetizers being passed by a server. "Are you hungry?"

Annie turned to look at him, then shook her head, waving away the waiter. "No, watching those two paw at each other made me lose my appetite."

The loud, upbeat music came to an end and a crowd of

people returned to their tables. The next song was slow, and he watched several couples step out onto the dance floor. "Well, then, would you care to dance? This would be a good opportunity for everyone at the tournament to see us together."

Annie eyed the people on the dance floor anxiously, then nodded with hesitation. "Okay. But you should know I'm a terrible dancer."

Nate laughed, reaching out a hand to her. "Somehow I find it hard to believe that you could be anything but graceful, Annie."

Her hand slipped into his, her soft velvet skin unusually cool as he clasped it. He squeezed it to warm her fingers as he led her gently into the center of the dance floor. With a turn, he wrapped an arm around her waist, his palm resting low on her bare back once again.

"That's it." He smiled down at her. "I'm buying you a new dress. Your hands are like ice."

Annie smiled with uncharacteristic nerves and shook her head. "It's not the dress," she admitted. "It's the dancing. I go cold when I'm nervous."

Nate couldn't help the look of surprise that spread across his face. His eyebrow arched high, his eyes narrowing at her. "The Barracuda, nervous? Never."

Annie was tough. She could take on every man in this room and beat them thoroughly. No doubt, she'd do it in stilettos and a skintight skirt. And yet the idea of dancing made her go cold in fear?

Annie wrinkled her nose and shifted in his arms, struggling to find a natural position. "Don't say that too loud." She leaned in. "It's one of my secret tells. All the players will come up with lame excuses to touch me if they think it will give away my bluff."

Nate chuckled, easing her into his arms, their bodies close but not quite touching. He wasn't sure he could take it if she pressed the full length of her against him.

Not here, at least.

He glanced around the room at the men watching them from the bar before meeting her unsure blue eyes. "Something tells me most of these men would need little excuse to touch you."

His firm hand guided them to the rhythm of the band playing. Annie was hesitant at first but fell easily into the motion. The song was slow with a slinky beat that the body couldn't help but respond to.

After a few moments, she leaned in and placed her head on his shoulder. Nate closed his eyes, hugging her closer and changing their motion to a subtle shifting of weight on his feet.

It felt so good to just hold her.

He leaned down to plant a kiss in the silky strands of her hair and breathed in deeply, letting the warm, seductive scent of her fill his senses. It was eerily familiar, like a distant memory he couldn't quite place and yet its name rested stubbornly on the tip of his tongue.

Annie was so soft in his arms. She fit there perfectly, as though her body had been made for him. It was the most comfortable feeling in the world, like slipping into a warm bath. He let himself submerge in the sensation.

Soon, the rest of the dancers, the musicians…even the room itself faded into nothingness. It was just Nate and Annie in each other's arms. Why did it feel as though he'd never held her like this before?

Perhaps because he hadn't. Yes, he'd made love to her. He'd explored every inch of her body. But never truly held her. Not like this. Annie was like a hummingbird, always flitting from one flower to the next. She was beautiful to look at, but you couldn't hold her. If you tried, she would vanish again. He'd learned that lesson the hard way.

Annie sighed, nestling deeper into his chest.

Nate's jaw tightened at the small cooing sound she made into his lapel. It was the same contented sound she made as she fell asleep. He remembered it in that instant. It had been so long since he'd heard it and at the same time, like yesterday that he'd made love to her.

The last night they were together she'd curled into a ball and had fallen asleep while he was in the shower. When he returned, he'd stood for a good half hour watching her sleep. He'd been mesmerized by her loveliness, her well-fortified facade wiped away by sleep. Her coal-black lashes had fluttered gently against her flushed cheeks, her kiss-swollen lips mouthing sleepy, confused words into her pillowcase.

His heart had nearly burst with pride when he realized she was his.

Nate had almost woken her up to make love to her again. If he'd known how quickly she would vanish from his life, he would've. He'd thought, foolishly, that he had all the time in the world to be with her and so had let her sleep.

Perhaps tonight he would make up for lost time and pick up where they'd left off.

He shouldn't have gone there. The instant heat flooded his groin, his body going from relaxed to uptight like the flick of a switch.

Annie noticed the sudden change as his body tensed, lifting her head to look at him with concern worrying her deep blue eyes. "What's wrong?"

The ballad came to an end, another upbeat song on its heels. People came and went on the dance floor, but Nate held them both in place. A slight shift of his body pressed the hard length of him against her stomach. "Nothing," Nate said with a wicked grin.

Annie's eyes grew wide before her lips twisted into a knowing smile. "I think we should go upstairs and do something about that."

Annie couldn't move fast enough. They said no good-byes as they made their way through the crowd and slipped out of the lounge. As the private elevator doors enclosed them, she turned to him, expecting him to de-vour her the moment they were finally alone.

Instead, Nate stuffed his hands in his pockets, leaning casually against the opposite wall. Despite his relaxed stance, his entire body was tense, his jaw flexed. His gaze penetrated her as it raked from top to bottom, but he didn't make a move except for a hard swallow that trav-eled down his throat to the buttoned collar of his tuxedo.

She'd forgotten how controlled he was. His gratifica-tion had always come from taking his time and enjoying every delicious second. Annie could never understand it. She was burning up for wanting him. She could feel the warmth between her thighs, the painful hardening of her nipples as her breasts tightened with desire. Her every nerve ached for the touch he denied.

She glanced down at the control panel. They still had fifteen floors to go. She couldn't wait that long. In one quick motion, Annie smacked the emergency button, bringing the elevator to a shaky, abrupt stop. Nate ad-justed his footing but didn't argue with her.

She looked him straight in the eye as she reached be-hind her neck and unfastened the halter of her dress. It was the only thing that held the dress on, so with a quick shimmy of her hips, the slinky blue fabric pooled to the floor. She stepped out of it, her eyes never leaving his dark gaze.

"Nate?" Gabe's voice barked at them from the two-way radio on Nate's belt.

Nate unclipped the radio, his gaze still fixed on Annie. "Yes?"

"We've got a report your elevator has stopped in between the tenth and eleventh floors."

His lips twisted in amusement as he pressed the button to respond. "That is correct."

There was a long silence before Gabe spoke again. "Okay, then. Radio if you need assistance."

"Will do." Nate turned the radio off and tossed it to the floor with a loud clank.

With the interruption behind them, Annie crossed the floor in two long strides and stopped just short of pressing her rock-hard nipples into his chest. He watched her, one hand still buried in his pocket, the other perched on his hip. She took a ragged breath and stared into the tensed muscles of his neck and jaw as they twitched beneath the skin. She ran her fingertip along the line of this throat, stopping at his collar.

Then she spoke. "Touch me, Nate. Don't make me wait any longer."

It was all that needed to be said. Nate's arms wrapped around her in an instant, pulling the full length of her body against him. His lips dipped down to brush against hers with a featherlight touch that sent a shiver of desire to the base of her spine.

"I want you," he whispered against her skin.

Annie answered with her lips, standing on her toes to reach up and capture his mouth. The kiss was tender at first, soothing the ache for a moment before the fire raged anew. Her fingers weaved into the blond curls at his neck, tugging him closer, but knowing he could never be close enough.

Nate's hands slid down her bare back, letting one dip lower to cup one lace-covered cheek. With a gentle squeeze, his hand continued down her silk-covered thigh to behind her knee, hitching her leg up to wrap around his waist.

Annie groaned as the new angle brought his erection into direct contact with her moist, aching sex. The sensation was overwhelming, and she knew it was just the beginning. Her mouth moved hard against his, her hands clawing at his tuxedo coat in a frenzy until he let it slip to the floor.

Her fingers were at his collar, undoing his shirt and thanking the heavens he wasn't wearing a tie for her to deal with. With his chest bare, she ran her hands over it, marveling at the hardened muscles she remembered. She let them dip lower and lower until the tips slid beneath the waist of his pants. She brushed the skin there, eliciting a groan and a sudden start as Nate grabbed her hand.

In one quick movement, he spun them around as though they were still on the dance floor. Now Annie was the one pinned against the wall, Nate pressing the length of his entire body against her. The brass was cold against her bare back, but she didn't care. It did little to soothe the fire that ran through her veins.

Nate's lips traveled from her jawline to her ear before moving slowly down her neck to the hollow of her throat. A tingle of anticipation coursed along her spine, her body shuddering at the searing caress of his mouth on her sensitive skin.

Annie tugged off his shirt and threw it to the floor. She wanted to keep her eyes open, to drink in the breathtaking sight of Nate, but she just couldn't. His mouth had traveled to the swell of her breasts. As he took one tight peach nipple into his mouth, her head flew back, her eyes closing on their own.

"Oh, Nate," she cried out, her fingers running through his golden curls, clutching his head and pulling him closer.

Oh, how she remembered this feeling. She'd suppressed the memory of it all these years, fearing she'd weaken and come back. Annie was addicted to him, addicted to how he could make her feel. As his hands and mouth slid over her skin, the craving burst to the surface once again.

Nate got down onto his knees, his lips nipping at her tensed stomach, his tongue circling her navel and dipping lower. Every muscle in her body tightened into knots when his hands brushed over the edge of her lace panties. She let go of his head to grip the railing and brace herself.

The panties came down inch by inch, the anticipation making her crazy until he eased up one leg, then the next, to cast them to the side. She was left wearing only her stockings and heels. Annie couldn't open her eyes. She was exposed, her trembling, aching body on display for him. If she looked at him, she might give herself away. She couldn't let him know just how badly she really wanted this. How long it had been...

His hands traveled from her ankles up the length of her silky stockings. Her legs trembled as he moved higher, his touch blazing a trail across her skin. She clutched the railing with all her might, her eyes squeezed shut, her bottom lip clamped between her teeth.

With gentle pressure, he eased her thighs apart, exposing her to the cool air before his warm breath tickled her skin. His fingers danced lazy circles up her thighs,

ANDREA LAURENCE   89

teasing her hip bones. Annie swallowed hard, her breath
caught in her chest as she waited.

Nate did not disappoint. He tasted her, drawing a
strained cry from her throat with its sudden attack. It
was followed by a second, then a more lingering caress
that was nearly enough to undo her. He must've sensed
it because he paused, giving her time to recover, then
continued his erotic assault on her body.

Annie cried out again, her hips straining to reach
for him. "Nathan, please," she panted. She wanted him.
Needed him. After three long years without his touch she
didn't want to wait another second to have him again.

"Please…*what*…Annie?" With each pause, his tongue
flicked over her.

"I want you inside me, Nate. Now, please." Annie
opened her eyes when the cold air tickled her skin.

He had moved to the other side of the elevator, undoing his belt and slipping out of his pants. He wasn't
looking down at his hands, though. He was looking at
her. Devouring her with his eyes. Annie could see him
mentally planning, the chess player in him working on
his next move.

She really didn't care what he did next as long as she
was covered by his massive warmth. He was just so beautiful. His body was even better than she remembered, as
though he'd spent the lonely nights since she'd left in the
hotel gym. Every inch of his body looked chiseled from
stone, the kind of male perfection that the great artists
of the Renaissance struggled to capture.

In one last move, his pants and briefs slid to the floor.
Instantly, he was as exposed as she was, his desire just as
obvious as it thrust proudly at her. Annie's breath caught
in her throat. Her lips were suddenly dry, forcing her to
snake her tongue across them.

Nate stepped out of his clothes and slowly walked back to her. Without a word, he circled his arms around her waist and lifted her up. She wrapped her legs around him and held his shoulders to keep her steady as he slowly lowered her onto him. He groaned, low and loud, as he was buried deep inside her.

They stood there, nearly still for a moment as they savored the sensation. It had been so long. She couldn't explain the feeling, but somehow it was so much more than just the physical pleasure of sex. There was a connection there that had never been broken. It had never wavered.

Nate eased her back against the wall, his hands cupping the swell of her bottom. His fingertips dug into her ample flesh. Slowly, agonizingly so, he withdrew and thrust forward, beginning an easy rhythm.

Annie clung to him, her face buried in his neck as he moved. With every movement, he went deeper and thrust harder, driving her closer and closer to the edge. His breath was hot and ragged in her ear, mingling with soft whispers she couldn't quite understand over her own cries.

She was nearly there, aching to go over the precipice, yet hesitant to let all this go. Her teeth gritted tight, her nails digging into his flexing shoulder blades. "Not yet," she panted. Annie wasn't ready to stop. She hadn't had enough of him yet.

She couldn't resist Nate. The rush of her addiction pumped through her veins, and the fears from her past slipped into her mind. This was why she had stayed so far away. She knew she wasn't strong enough. She couldn't deny him her body when it was all she wanted to give him.

Nate was not deterred by her apparent refusal. He widened his stance, gripping her with almost crushing strength to thrust in short, quick movements that left her no choice in the matter. The pressure built up, washing over her like a tidal wave. She was swept up in it, overwhelmed by the sensations she had deprived herself of for so long.

"Yes," Nate hissed into her ear, coaxing her release as he held her thrashing body tight against him. When she stilled, softening in his arms from exhaustion, he moved quickly, shouting out her name with his last few thrusts.

Exhausted, he eased her back against the wall, resting her bottom on the railing. It was cold, but Annie didn't care. Her whole body was throbbing, her skin feverish and slick with sweat.

Nate propped his elbows on the wall beside her and leaned against it to breathe, his body still cradled between her trembling thighs. "That—" he spoke between rapid breaths "—was worth the wait, but let's not go another three years before we do it again." His dark eyes studied her face for a moment before he lifted her up off the railing. With her wrapped around him, he reached over to hit the button and let the elevator continue up to his suite.

Seven

Annie wasn't certain how the first day of the tournament would go. She was used to playing on her own terms. Free to indulge her superstitious rituals without personal distractions. This mess was the opposite of how she liked to work.

For one, she got almost no sleep. She and Nate had made love until her muscles gave out and she simply couldn't do anything but collapse onto the bed. When she finally did sleep, it was like a minicoma until Nate shook her shoulder and told her she had to get up.

It felt odd to wake up in Nate's bed with him beside her. Strangely comforting and familiar. She didn't remember this feeling from before. Then there had only been the panic of knowing she was married. Today she was still married, but that didn't seem to bother her as much.

It was an interesting and unsettling development. She'd sat up in bed and watched him disappear down the hall in nothing but pajama pants. Almost immediately her body was ready for more of him, but she knew now was the time to focus. She had a big day ahead of her.

Before she could go downstairs, she had to get briefed

by Gabe for the tenth time. She also had to get wired.
That experience itself was uncomfortable enough, even
with Nate's warm hands under her blouse to distract her.
The head of security had said several important things
after that, but all she knew was that the tape that secured
the wires pulled at her skin and itched something fierce.
She still hadn't adjusted to the idea of having Gabe listening in to her conversations all day. Same team or no,
every word out of her mouth was subject to his scrutiny
and she didn't like having to worry about it on top of
everything else.

Add all that onto the pressure of scoping out her fellow players and she was completely unprepared to play
poker. With the way she felt, she might just choke and get
eliminated before she could fulfill her end of the bargain
with Nate. What would his price be then?

Annie settled into her assigned seat and eyed Gordon
Barker. He was three seats down. Gabe had arranged for
her to share a table with him today because he was on
their short list of suspects. She'd heard a rumor or two
about him over the years, but they'd never been as loud
as the ones about someone like Eddie Walker. If he was
involved in some elaborate scheme, he was smart enough
to keep it quiet.

Personally, Annie hadn't had a lot of experience playing with him, so she wasn't sure either way. As the tournament started, she decided to spend the first few hands
focused on her game and building her chips. Once she
had a healthy cushion above the other players, she would
feel more comfortable breaking her focus to watch Gordon. She had to play well if she was going to be successful in any of this.

As the lunch break approached, Annie was pleased
with how the day had gone. A few players had been elim-

inated. Gordon was still playing, but she'd seen nothing suspicious and she hadn't lost any hands to him. He was probably another name she could cross off the list, but she wasn't about to rule him out yet. If she was too good at her job, soon there wouldn't be anyone but Eddie on Nate's radar. Toppling him would not only be difficult, but destructive. Tessa would not be happy if she found out Annie had sent her boyfriend to jail.

When the tournament stopped for lunch, she grabbed her food and went to sit down beside the Captain. She figured he was probably her safest bet for company. He wasn't much for gossip. With any luck, she could attempt to make conversation and dig for information as required, but he wouldn't deliver anything but another one of his long-winded Navy stories. It was the perfect choice.

"Afternoon, *Mrs. Reed.* How's your game going today?"

Annie smiled and shrugged. "Too early to tell."

"Don't let yourself get distracted by thoughts of that handsome husband of yours. You two seem to be enjoying this second honeymoon of sorts, but it can mess with your game. It's no coincidence that every time I won the championship, I was between marriages."

She opened her bag of chips and let a smile curl her lips. The Captain always seemed to be between marriages. She'd lost count at six. Her one marriage was too much for her to handle. "I'll try. I'm worried about Gordon Barker, though. I've heard rumors he doesn't play a fair game. I'd hate to get bumped out because he's dirty."

The Captain shook his head and took a bite of his sandwich. "You don't need to worry about Gordon. He's been clean for years. Had a brush with the law that was a little too close for comfort a while back and he straightened right out."

"Oh," Annie said. Well, at least the conversation was

getting her somewhere and Gabe couldn't accuse her of not doing her job. She was hoping to string Gordon along as an option for a while longer, but now she could focus on the rest of her game instead of him. "That's a relief."

"You'll want to watch out for Eddie Walker, though."

Annie stopped, her bottle of water hovering in midair. She hadn't expected this at all, but she should've known the Captain would want to look out for her. He'd been the closest thing she'd had to a father over the years. "He's not at my table today."

"Well, the problem with Eddie is that he works with a circle of players and dealers. It's actually better if he's at your table because he always keeps his own game clean. He's a tricky bastard. I wish to God someone would catch him so we wouldn't have to deal with the scrutiny. It messes with my game to know how many security people are circling around and watching my every play."

She immediately felt guilty for talking with him while wearing a wire. "I'm surprised no one has caught him yet, given how many people know about it."

"He's careful. And smart. There's one main player they try to push through to the final table and a good ten or more in the tournament just to help them along. You never know who's in on it. I heard he's got a new partner working with him this year. I haven't seen her myself," he continued. "But I heard she's—"

She? Annie sucked a sip of her bottled water into her lungs accidentally, launching into a mad coughing fit. The Captain immediately stopped talking and patted her on the back, watching with concern as she wheezed and viciously hacked.

"Are you okay?" he asked when several minutes had passed and the bright red faded from her face.

"Yes, I'm sorry." She nodded. "If you'll excuse me, I think I'll run to the ladies' room."

"Of course."

At that, Annie dashed away to the safety of the rest-room and hoped Gabe's security goons had the good sense to stop listening in.

With the way the tournament play fell, Annie was scheduled Saturday so she had Sunday off. They had a record number of registrations, so the breakup allowed everyone to participate. The numbers dwindled exponentially after that point, so the top players from Saturday and Sunday would then combine to continue on Monday.

In theory, Nate should've been down on the casino floor making sure everything was going as planned, but he just couldn't make himself do it. Saturday had been agony. He'd watched Annie play from a distance all afternoon, unable to touch her the way he ached to. His fists had been curled tight in his pockets for hours, a fake smile plastered onto his face.

When she finished for the day, victorious, he'd whisked Annie away to the suite. She'd barely been able to bask in the glory of her poker domination before she was naked and writhing under him again. They'd spent the entire evening holed up in the suite, ordering room service and making love on every piece of furniture he owned.

As the sunlight began pouring in the windows Sunday morning, Nate rolled onto his side and stared down at her. She looked as though he had thoroughly exhausted her. The long strands of her dark hair were messy and sprawled across the pillow, her eyes dancing under her lids with dreaming.

Throwing back the covers, he disappeared silently

down the hallway. By the time he reached his desk, he could hear the chattering music of his smartphone. It was Gabe's ringtone. He hadn't spoken to him since the end of tournament play yesterday. He was certain his head of security had been anticipating a daily debrief with Annie, but Nate hadn't felt like sharing her last night.

"Hey," he answered.

"Good morning, sunshine," Gabe said dryly. "We need to talk about something that happened yesterday."

Nate frowned and settled into his desk chair. "What?"

"I was down on the floor watching Eddie as you directed, but one of my guys, Stuart, was doing surveillance and listening to Annie's conversations."

He didn't really want to know what his friend would say next. It would ruin his sex buzz. "And?" he said reluctantly.

"She was talking to the Captain and having a fairly blunt conversation about Walker. He indicated that he'd heard Walker had recruited a new woman to work with him. Just when he was about to elaborate, Annie went into a mad coughing fit and immediately dismissed herself."

That wasn't good. Knowing the accomplice was a woman reduced the suspect list dramatically. Knowing Annie had abruptly ended the conversation, hadn't followed up and hadn't passed any information on to him or Gabe narrowed it to a party of one. Was it possible that Tessa was more than just Eddie's girlfriend? Could she be involved in the cheating, as well, or was the Captain just misinformed? He needed to get Annie away from the casino and all the intrusions.

"I think I'm going to take Annie to the house today. We both know Eddie is up to something, possibly Tessa, as well, but I'm not sure about what Annie knows. I was thinking I could get more information out of her if we're away from the casino."

"Make sure you don't get played. You don't know how involved she is with all this. For all we know, she's the ringleader and using her relationship with you as a diversion."

"I guess we'll find out." At that, Nate hit the button to disconnect the call. He didn't like thinking about Annie like that. He would do what was smart, but he hesitated to be instantly suspicious of her like Gabe.

Flipping through his address book, he punched in a name and within seconds had his housekeeper, Ella, on the phone. The older woman was in her late fifties and lived exclusively at Nate's house. She kept the place clean and organized. If he decided to do something at the house, Ella would make sure everything was taken care of.

He explained his plans and she was all too eager to prepare everything for their arrival. Honestly, he hadn't been back to the house in more than a month. The poor woman was probably bored to tears and suddenly all atwitter as she readied the house.

"Nate?" Annie's sleepy voice called to him from the bedroom.

Nate switched off his phone and headed back to her. "Good, you're up," he said and sat on the edge of the bed. "Get dressed."

"You mean you're going to keep your hands to yourself long enough for me to put clothes on?" Annie sat up in bed, the navy sheets clutched to her bare chest.

Nate eyed her for a moment—the sexy mess of her hair over her shoulders, the smooth length of her leg peeking out from beneath the covers, the full swell of her breasts pressed against her arms. That was a very good question. He was considering having her again before they left. The only thing stopping him was the opportunity to make love to her someplace new.

"Only if you hurry." He grinned and disappeared into the closet.

They did hurry, hopping into his convertible Mercedes as the valet pulled it around. Within minutes, they left the bustle of the Strip behind and settled into the sprawling suburbia that surrounded it. He'd told Annie to dress casually and bring a swimsuit. He expected her to ask questions, but she seemed content to watch the scenery go by.

It took about twenty minutes to get to his subdivision. The two-story Spanish-style house was typical for the area, with the sand-colored stucco walls and red clay tile roof. The yard was well landscaped but lacked any sort of personality. It could've been anyone's house. Were it not at the very end of the cul-de-sac, it might've been hard for even Nate to pick it out from the others.

Nate hit the button to open the garage and pulled in beside the empty spot where Ella's green Buick normally parked. He felt bad about the sudden plans, so he'd sweetened the deal with the offer of an afternoon of pampering at the Sapphire Spa. She deserved it. It also got her out from underfoot. Ella didn't know about his marriage to Annie and he wanted it to stay that way.

Nate sighed and opened the door. "I'd give you the tour, but I'm a little rusty on it myself."

Annie chuckled, scooping her purse off the floor and climbing out of the car. "You really need to focus on some work-life balance, Nate."

He held his arms out wide. "I'm here, aren't I?" He fished the keys out of his khaki shorts and unlocked the door. "Besides, I'm not taking any criticisms from a woman that lives out of her suitcase."

"Touché." She smiled, slipping past him into the dark, empty house.

As promised, the tour was short. They made a pit stop in the master suite to christen the king-size bed, then slipped into their swimsuits and took a dip in the cool turquoise pool in the backyard. Like children, they splashed each other and roughhoused in the water, then ambitiously napped in lounge chairs until the rumbling of their empty stomachs distracted them.

Without room service to call on, they wandered into the kitchen to see what Ella had left for them. An ivory note card on the counter informed them about the fixings for homemade pizza in the refrigerator.

"Do you think we can handle this?" Annie looked dubiously at the ball of dough on the counter.

"Oh, come on," Nate prodded, scooping an armful of food off the shelf. "Certainly we can manage a pizza. Ella's already done most of the work. It will be fun to try, at least. If it's a disaster, we can order something later. Here." He slid a few tomatoes and a pouch of fresh basil across the granite countertop. "You get the toppings for the pizza ready while I work on the dough."

Nate assembled the pizza, ladling Ella's homemade sauce and spreading fresh mozzarella slices on the crust. He watched Annie out of the corner of his eye as she worked busily, cutting tomatoes. She looked really beautiful today. Yes, she looked sexy almost all of the time, but most definitely beautiful now. The pool had washed away all traces of her makeup. Her long dark hair was still damp, the thick, corded strands running down her bare back. Her golden skin seemed even darker against the stark white of her bikini. She'd wrapped a colorful cotton fabric around her waist, tying it in a knot slung low at her hip bone. It hid the tiny white string bikini bottoms she'd pressed against him in the pool.

She caught him watching her and she smiled, giggling in a girlish way that made his chest ache unexpectedly. Annie away from the casino was like a new person. She didn't just look different, she acted different. In only a few hours' time, he'd gotten to see a more casual, easy-going version of her. He liked this Annie even more than his superconfident but guarded card shark.

But that wasn't all of it. There was something familiar and soothing about the banality of their actions. Making lunch together in his house away from the casino…it was more significant a moment than he'd expected.

Yes, making love to her again had been great, but this kind of experience seemed important in a different way. They'd never had any real domestic moments together. Suddenly that bothered him more than he wanted it to. They'd never had a real marriage. They'd just had some fantasy honeymoon that existed only within the walls of his hotel. His work quickly became her prison. Making lunch, watching television, even grocery shopping were things they'd never experienced together and it made him sad. Perhaps they would've had a shot if they'd done this three years ago.

This week was supposed to be about making Annie miserable and finally being able to put her out of his mind for good, but he wasn't getting over Annie as he'd planned. The more he had her, the more he wanted of her. He should've just signed the divorce papers instead of luring her back here.

"You have sauce on your cheek."

Nate looked up, his thoughts disturbed. "What?"

Annie reached out and wiped a dab of renegade marinara off his face. She licked it off her finger and smiled. "Ella makes wonderful tomato sauce."

"She does. It makes me want to stay at the house more often so she can cook for me all the time."

"Why don't you?"

Nate shrugged, scooping a few tomato slices off the counter and scattering them on the pizza. The answer was that there was really nothing to come home to. Work always needed him. This empty house, not so much. If he'd had a family, it would be a different story. "No real reason to be here, I suppose."

"Then why do you have a house?"

"I bought it when the market was low, so it's a good investment. Someplace to go when I need to get away from work. And…" He hesitated before completing the thought. "I'd hoped that I'd get married one day and have a family here." He looked up at Annie with a playful grin. "That hasn't quite panned out for me yet."

Annie uneasily matched his grin, quickly turning back to slicing the last of the tomato and starting on the basil. "So if you never come here, Nate, why exactly did we make this little field trip today?"

Nate stilled over the pizza. He'd been waiting for the right moment, enjoying his afternoon with Annie too much to ruin it. But she'd opened the door. It was time. "I wanted to bring you here to ask you something."

Annie frowned slightly. "Sounds ominous."

"I guess it depends on your answer." He shrugged. "I wanted to get you away from the casino, the tournament and the wires recording your every word in the hopes I could get an honest answer out of you."

Nate laid the last of the tomato slices onto the pizza. "I'm worried about the conversation you had with the Captain about Eddie. If Eddie really is working with a woman, the list of partners dwindles significantly. You can imagine what my concern is." He paused, watching her look down at the herbs to avoid his gaze. "Hit me with some basil."

Annie's expression was neutral as she sprinkled the leaves across the pizza and dusted her hands together to brush the remaining bits into the sink. "You think Tessa might be more than just his flavor of the month?"

"It's a scenario we have to consider. She is registered in the tournament."

"And you're worried I won't cooperate in convicting my own sister."

Leave it to Annie to cut to the chase. "I hope it doesn't come down to that, but yes. Gabe is concerned that you can't be trusted to bring us information if it might implicate her. Or even that you might try to use our relationship as a distraction to protect Tessa."

"And you? Are you suspicious of me, too?"

Nate turned and looked her directly in the eye. "Yes. It would be stupid not to at least consider it as a possibility." A flicker of emotion ran across Annie's face, but it was too quick for Nate to detect whether it was guilt, pain or irritation.

"Let me ease a couple of your concerns," she began. "First, *you* came to *me* with this arrangement, so you can hardly accuse me of manipulating the situation to protect or distract attention from Tessa. Two, my sister and I aren't very close. She doesn't confide in me, so if you think I have any inside knowledge into what she's doing, you're wrong. If I had any evidence of her or anyone else cheating, I'd turn it over so I could focus on my game and stop wearing that itchy damn wire.

"And finally," she said, reaching a hand up to cup his cheek and looking him directly in the eyes, "I'm sleeping with you because I want to. You're the sexiest man I've ever encountered and I can't help but want you."

Nate's chest tightened. He didn't know if it was her brutally honest answers or the way she looked at him when she said how badly she wanted him. Before he could reach out to her, she pulled away to scoop up the pizza stone and carry it to the oven. Annie slid the pizza stone inside and shut the heavy stainless-steel door. "How long does it bake for?"

Nate examined the card Ella had left for them. "She says about fifteen to twenty minutes but that we should watch for the crust to brown."

She set the digital clock for twenty minutes. "Okay, that's done, so I'm going to hop in the shower."

With that, she turned and sauntered out of the kitchen, the colorful wrap falling seductively from her hips to the tile floor.

Annie hadn't been surprised by Nate's questions. She'd been caught off guard by the Captain's words at lunch the day before, which was why she'd choked, but her fears about it being true were why she hadn't returned to follow up. She didn't want to turn in Tessa. And she would go to great lengths to avoid uncovering her sister's involvement. But at this moment, she had absolutely no evidence of anything but her sister's poor choices in men and no problem telling Nate as much.

Her answers seemed to satisfy him. For now.

When she got out of the shower, Nate had taken the pizza and a pitcher of iced tea out onto the covered patio. They dined, then moved to the poolside chairs. Annie lay out on her stomach and was very nearly asleep when she felt Nate's gaze on her. She opened one eye toward him, wincing at the sunlight despite her fashionably over-sized sunglasses.

He was openly appraising her body, his jaw hard set in restraint as he took in the dark expanse of her skin. When he realized she was watching him, he smiled sheepishly. "Your body should be bare and sun-kissed more often. It belongs on the white sand beaches of the Caribbean. Not in a dark, smoke-filled casino."

Although Nate hadn't specifically said it, Annie's brain immediately went to being on that beach with him. Being here with Nate had been an eye-opening experience, to say the least. She'd been given a glimpse, how-ever small, of what life with him could be like. Life away from the casino. Just him and her living their lives to-gether the way they'd first envisioned.

Annie had expected their time together to be uncom-fortable. Nate had made it perfectly clear that he'd wanted her to suffer. Adding sex to the mix had changed their dynamic, but she still anticipated the panic to come even-tually. The urge to run. Now she was envisioning herself in a hammock swinging in the breeze on the beach *with him*. She didn't feel oppressed. She didn't feel tied down. She actually felt…great. Which was terrible.

"There isn't much money to be made on a beach." She rolled onto her back and smiled at him. "I follow the tournaments. If there's not a casino to host one, I prob-ably won't go there."

Nate frowned at her. "So you never just take a vaca-tion for the sake of vacation? No break from cards and casinos?"

Annie shrugged and closed her eyes. "Not really. I travel so much as it is that I don't exactly relish the idea of traveling just to spend money instead of making it."

"What about as a kid? Didn't your family ever go on trips to Florida or the Grand Canyon?"

"As a child, I saw almost every corner of this country, but not to vacation. We just moved all the time. My mother was on this constant journey, looking for something that she never found. To this day, I still don't know what it was."

"What about your father?"

Annie tried to shrug dismissively, but it wasn't convincing. "She left him behind. Apparently I wasn't important enough for him to chase after. And even if he'd wanted to, she would've vanished again."

"So that's where you get it?"

Annie frowned. She hated her childhood. Hated growing up never keeping friends or a real home. Being compared to her mother wasn't exactly the highest compliment in her eyes.

"I suppose so," she admitted. She knew what he meant. Through someone else's eyes, she supposed she looked flighty. And part of her was. When she was of age, her inner nomad had immediately taken over and she'd nearly become as bad as her mother. She fought it, maintaining a home in Miami and finding a line of work where she filled the urge by traveling a lot. But there was a difference. She was alone, doing what she pleased. She'd never subject a child to her lifestyle. Or a husband.

"Why did I have to marry a woman with a long family history of nomadic male abandonment?"

"You should never fall for a gypsy, Nate. It always ends badly."

"I'll take that under consideration, though I might suggest that in the future you throw that line out on the first date."

Annie rolled her eyes and lay back into the chair. "It

sounds like you're the one that needs a vacation. You've been killing yourself at that casino for years."

"I was thinking about it. My family owns a house on St. Thomas. I haven't been there since I was a kid, but it might be time. Where are you off to after this?"

"I have another tournament in a few weeks, so I'll be heading up to Vancouver, then Monte Carlo a month after that. Not quite a vacation, but it's my first chance to see Monaco."

Nate perked up in his chair. "Monte Carlo? I've always wanted to see the Formula One race. It's in early May, around when you're going, but I'm always too busy to get away."

He hadn't said he wanted to go with her, but Annie sensed an interest she didn't expect. She never imagined that Nate would follow her anywhere, especially for something as insignificant as a poker tournament. She'd always envisioned their marriage inside the sphere of the Sapphire, as though they were both trapped within a snow globe. That was the way he'd seemed to like it back then. He didn't want to leave and he certainly didn't want Annie leaving without him. It definitely changed her outlook on things to know he was branching out.

Annie sighed, shifting the uncomfortable subjects from her mind. It was easy to do. The warmth of the sun was so soothing, soaking into her bones. "I don't want to go back to the hotel. Can't we just stay here?"

Nate chuckled beside her, a low rumble on the breeze. "That does sound tempting, but it's hard to win a tournament that way. Even for someone as talented as you are."

Annie laughed and closed her eyes. "Ruin all my fun, why don't you?"

All this talk of vacations was just that...talk. Here, away from the troubles that surrounded them, it seemed possible. But once they returned to the Sapphire, she was certain it would fly out the window. If he was right and her sister was involved, their reunion was just a ticking time bomb. Annie was sure if she didn't leave first, Nate would be the one to push her away.

She wasn't certain she could stand mourning this relationship a second time.

Eight

Nate was tired of the tournament already and they still had three days to go. Hosting it was good business, but now that he had Annie in his bed, the tournament and the chaos that surrounded it could disappear for all he cared.

He eyed his watch impatiently. There were two hours left of play today. Annie was doing well. She'd already single-handedly eliminated three people at her table. Before long, she would move on to another.

He'd tried not to hover. There were dozens of tables to watch and VIPs to entertain, but he kept wandering back in her direction. She had a gravitational force that seemed to impact only him. No matter how hard he tried to pull away, she'd draw him back to her. If he'd been smart, he would've left a few hundred miles between them. Now he had no way to fight it.

And he no longer wanted to.

Nate needed to focus. His short list of potential cheaters required his attention. Annie was watching another player at her table today, but she'd muttered under her breath into the wire that it was another dead end. He wasn't about to give up, though. An entire team of security staff was watching the tables from overhead security cameras in addition to the people on the floor. A couple were plainclothes, but most were in the standard navy blazers with earpieces that gave them away. Gabe had been assigned to watch Eddie. A few of his best guys were assigned various other people, which now included Tessa.

As much as Annie insisted she would turn over her sister if necessary, he knew she wouldn't go out of her way to collect evidence against her, either. If she was more than just Eddie's girlfriend, his team would have to be the ones to uncover it.

Annie's laughter called to him over the chaos of the room. He turned, drawn back to her. She looked so lovely today. Her shiny dark hair hung loose around her face. Her vivid purple blouse was clingy and unbuttoned low enough to give all the players an ample view. She knew it, too, leaning forward innocently onto the table. If she wasn't careful, someone might see the tiny black microphone nestled between her breasts.

Nate's jaw tightened. He knew it was simply a part of her game strategy, but that didn't mean he had to like it. They might not have much of a marriage, but they were telling people they had reconciled. Seducing her opponents at the table didn't do much for their cover. If it was even a cover anymore. His pangs of jealousy felt real. The lines had become terribly blurred lately.

He took a deep breath and tried to focus on her game. The other player went all in. Nate watched, knowing Annie wouldn't give away a single thing. Her face was serenely calm, her lips parted in a smile that would confuse any man. She sat for a second, mentally calculating her hand and how best to play it. The cards on the table didn't give much away.

Annie's fingernails ran down a stack of chips, counting them out, and then she tossed them onto the pile in the center. Both players flipped their cards, but Nate didn't get to see them. It wasn't until he saw the man shake Annie's hand and walk from the table that he knew *the Barracuda* had claimed another victim. Nate tried not to smile, but he couldn't help it. He was beaming with pride. His wife was beautiful and talented, and everyone knew it.

His wife.

Nate stopped in his tracks when he realized what he'd just thought. His mouth went dry. Despite being legally married the past three years, Nate had never really thought of Annie as his wife. He'd barely adjusted to the idea of being married when she left. Then she'd simply become *"her."* But now…now that he knew she had one foot out the door of his life, never to return…now he decided to stake this mental claim to her?

He'd thought he had done well to compartmentalize this week and what it really meant—nothing but some great goodbye sex. Focusing on their physical connection was the smart choice. It was the piece that had always worked between them. But recently, it was not Annie's naked body or cries of passion that occupied his thoughts. He'd started thinking beyond the tournament and the potential for more.

He glanced across the tables to where Annie was sitting. He wanted to ask her to stay. To give them another shot at the relationship they never really tried. But what would she say if he asked? Nate had felt them growing closer, felt her letting down her guard, but would it be what drove her away?

This was definitely not what he'd had in mind when he hauled her to his suite and blackmailed her into helping him.

"Mr. Reed?" A voice chirped over his radio.

Nate unclipped it immediately and moved away from the crowd for privacy. "Yes?"

"Sir, we've detained someone in the security office. Gabe has requested your attendance."

Nate frowned and cast a quick glance over to where Tessa had been sitting. She was still there, her flame-red hair giving her away. Richard, one of the senior security agents, was still watching her, and another security agent had taken Gabe's place watching Eddie.

He breathed a sigh of relief. "I'll be right there," he answered. Hopefully they'd get a break that wouldn't involve his sister-in-law. That would make everything easier.

When he arrived in the security office, he found Gabe sitting at a table in the conference room with someone he didn't recognize. The guy was short, thick through the middle, with pudgy fingers, greasy gray hair and a bristly beard. He was older, in his late fifties, maybe.

His eyes widened when he caught a glimpse of Nate standing in the doorway. He'd opened his mouth to argue something with Gabe, but froze, clamping his mouth tightly shut.

"Mr. Hansen," Nate greeted Gabe officially. "Who do we have the pleasure of meeting with today?"

"Mr. Reed, this is Keith Frye. Mr. Frye was participating in the tournament downstairs. It seems our cards weren't good enough for him and he felt it necessary to bring a couple of his own."

"I just wanted to—"

"That's fine, Mr. Frye," Nate interrupted. "We understand. Some people prefer to use their own, especially when they're better than the ones the dealer provides." He turned to Gabe. "Do we have everything we need?"

"Yes, sir. The overhead camera has clear film of him slipping cards from his pocket into his hand. We'll notify the authorities as soon as we're done here."

"Excellent." Nate was pleased things were under control but slightly curious as to why he had been summoned up for something this trivial. Yes, he liked to know everything that went on in his casino, but Gabe normally handled things like this on his own.

"I'm not the only one!" Keith blurted out as Nate turned to walk out.

Now they were getting somewhere. Nate met Gabe's grin with interest and returned. "Continue."

"He said it might help me out." He flipped a thumb in Gabe's direction.

"Might," Nate emphasized. "Let's hear what you've got first."

Keith looked down at his hands, nervously picking at his fingernails. "There's this guy, Darrell. I don't know his last name. A couple nights ago I was hanging out in the bar, having a few drinks, when Darrell and some other guy I don't know sat down at a table near me."

There wasn't a Darrell on his list of suspects. "Do you know this Darrell guy?"

"No, but he had a blue dealer's vest folded up beside him, and the guy he met up with called him Darrell."

Nate clamped his teeth together to keep from yelling at the man in frustration. That was why. He was a dealer, not a player. He hated to think that one of his own employees was involved in something like this, but it was inevitable.

"So these guys start talking about the tournament and what they're planning to do. They were sorta speaking around what they really meant, but I could follow along well enough. I pretended I wasn't listening, but it was easy to hear with them sitting so close."

"And?" Nate was anxious to hear the rest of this convoluted tale.

"And they sounded like they were plotting something. Arranging who was going to do what. Sounded like this Darrell guy was messing with the cards. That's where I got the idea, you see? It sounded like there were several people in on it. Other dealers, other players. Even some chick."

Nate perked up. "Some chick?"

"Yeah, she came into the bar later. They'd been talking about her on and off, but then this redhead strolls in and the other guy left with her."

Nate's stomach sank. A redhead. Every word out of this guy's mouth seemed to put another nail into the coffin of his future with Annie. "What did the other guy look like? The one Darrell was talking to?"

"Kinda skinny. Dark hair. He was wearing a Dallas Cowboys windbreaker. The girl was hot. Pretty tall for a girl. Nice rack."

Nate swallowed the lump in his throat. There was no question he was talking about Eddie and Tessa. "Anything else?"

"No, that's about it. So, hey, was that good enough to cut me some slack with the cops?"

He thrust his fists into his pockets and nodded. "Yeah. You leave your personal information with security here, in case we have any questions, and you'll be free to go. I'm sure the money you lost paying to enter the tournament will be punishment enough. If I ever see you back in this casino again, I won't be as lenient, Mr. Frye."

Nate turned to Gabe. "Find me this Darrell guy's personnel file. And see if you can find footage from that night in the lounge. I'm heading up to my office."

Gabe gave him a curt nod and continued filling out the forms on the table.

Nate spun on his heel and disappeared from the conference room. He needed to get out of there. Get away from the guy who had given them their big break in the worst possible way. He blew down the hallway, his friendly demeanor gone. Employees dodged out of his way as he stomped to the elevator and up to his suite.

He was pounding mercilessly on his laptop when the elevator chimed. Nate looked up, anticipating Gabe with the file he'd requested, but it was Annie.

She came over to him, dropping her purse onto the sofa and sitting on the edge of his desk to face him. Her pink grin was wide, born of confidence. She'd no doubt slaughtered the competition today. Her sapphire eyes searched his scowling face for a moment before the light in her expression dimmed. "What's wrong?"

Nate swallowed and looked down at her knee. He let his hand roam over the bare skin, distracting himself with the silky touch of her. "Work stuff," he said. He would leave it at that until he was certain there was something more to say. He wanted solid, convictable evidence on Tessa first.

"Aww," she cooed, slipping off the desk and circling his black leather executive chair. She leaned over the back, her fingers kneading at the tense muscles of his shoulders.

Her touch was enough to chase away all his dark thoughts. Her hands worked on the knots and nerves like a skilled masseuse. It was unnerving how she knew just how to touch him, just what he needed. There was a comfort in her mere presence that made the stress of his day not seem as important anymore.

"You know what you need? A dip in the spa." Annie walked out of the room, various articles of her clothing left in her wake. Nate shrugged out of his coat and tie, following the crumbs Annie left to the balcony.

The secluded balcony was off the large glass wall of the living room and overlooked the hotels across the strip. It had an in-ground spa, a fully stocked bar, a luxurious outdoor living room set, a fire pit and even a putting green. It was the perfect place for a party or an interlude for two. At least that was the idea. He almost never came out here.

A chrome-and-glass overhang and a few well-placed trees in glazed clay pots provided ample privacy, with a latticed alcove around the sunken Whirlpool. It was a necessity with the child-friendly Excalibur Hotel so close. Anyone with binoculars and an inclination could see onto the patio from the right hotel room.

Nate slid through the glass door and turned the corner just in time to see Annie's round, firm behind slip into the swirling, hot water. She'd clipped her hair up into a messy bun on the top of her head, but a few strands still trailed over her shoulders. He unbuttoned his shirt slowly, his eyes glued to her bare back as it disappeared beneath the surface.

With the water up to her shoulder blades, Annie turned and sat facing him. The steam from the water had dampened the loose tendrils around her face and gave her cheeks a rosy glow. She smiled at him, the cheerful pink lipstick ready and waiting for him to remove it.

"Well, come on," she urged.

Nate complied, tugging off his shirt, throwing it to the patio floor and following it with the rest of his clothes. He could barely feel the scalding water as he stepped into it. He was focused only on Annie. Even with his suspicion of her sister lingering overhead, he needed to touch her. His body demanded it.

He didn't bother sitting. Instead, Nate crouched low into the water and moved across to kneel in front of her. His hands pried her thighs apart, giving him a place to nestle in against her.

She moved in, wrapping her legs around his waist and tugging him closer. With a quick spin, he lifted her with him until he was the one sitting and she was straddling his lap.

"Mmm…" She sighed, pressing against him. "So, would you like to talk about your bad day?"

Nate smiled, gliding the length of him back and forth across her most sensitive parts. "What bad day?"

Annie ground her hips against him, closing her eyes to allow herself to fully experience the sensations coursing through her body. It amazed her how quickly and easily he could bring her to the edge. It seemed to take almost no effort at all on his part, making her wonder once again if he'd been given the instruction manual to her body.

In her new position, her breasts were easily within reach of his mouth. He didn't hesitate to lean forward and run his tongue through the valley in between. Nate turned his cheek, planting a kiss on the side of her breast, then continuing down around the edge of it. His caresses moved lazily around her hardened nipple, coming close but not touching the place she ached for him the most.

Nate continued to lick and nibble at her sensitive flesh as his hands slid down her back and cupped her rear. He guided the motions of her hips, sliding the length of him along her sex in such a way that coaxed her nerve endings to tingle from her fingertips to her toes and yet denied her the contact she craved.

Annie bit her bottom lip, struggling to catch enough friction, but he was stronger than she was. He was going to drag this out as long as he could.

"It's just too much temptation for you," he murmured against her breast.

Before Annie could respond, he took one nipple into his mouth and sucked hard. She cried out, her answer forgotten as the pleasure stabbed sharp through her. Her hips bucked against him, seeking out what she needed and failing once again.

In one fluid motion Nate stood, lifting her up out of the water and sending a wave over the side of the spa that soaked the surrounding concrete. She clamored quickly to wrap her arms around his neck, but he immediately sat her on the opposite edge of the Whirlpool.

He knelt in front of her, his mouth still tightly clamped onto her aching breast. Annie arched her back, clutching his damp blond curls and pressing against the hardened muscles of his stomach.

Nate let go of her breast at last, giving the tip of her nipple a quick flick with his tongue, then moving back to kiss her sternum, grazing down her stomach. He leaned into her then, forcing her backward until her shoulders met with the cool stone of the patio. His body nearly covered hers, and she pulled her legs up to cradle his body. She smiled, thinking perhaps she would finally get what she was after.

Instead, he pulled away, leaving a trail of kisses down her stomach. The muscles of her belly quivered with need, his mouth tickling and torturing her as he moved lower. She didn't know if she could take much more of this. He would tease and taunt her with his hands and his mouth until she'd agree to nearly anything.

It was unfair. As many times as he'd had her since that first night, she'd hardly been given the opportunity to reciprocate. He was so intently focused on her and her pleasure, it was hard to complain. But he was the one who needed the attention today, not her.

"Nate?" Annie whimpered, her whole body trembling with wanting him. "Nate?" she said again with more force when he didn't answer.

He paused, his lips hovering just above her dark, cropped curls, his hooded eyes watching her over the hills and valleys of her exposed body. "Yes?"

Annie took advantage of his hesitation to sit up and make a futile attempt to push his shoulders back. "I want my turn." She gave him a sly grin and slid into the water. Her eyes stayed intently focused on him as her lips took their turn to run down his stomach, her hands gently caressing and kneading his tensed muscles.

Nate was so tall that when he was standing, his erection rose proudly above the waterline. It brushed against Annie's breasts as she sank into the water, eliciting a shudder from him.

She took advantage, letting one hardened nipple run over the tip, then drag down the length of him. Annie smiled when she saw Nate's fists curl tightly at his sides. This was the only way she knew of to get Nate to lose control. He was always so calculating, so in command of his world. Here, now, Annie was the one in charge.

Without giving him time to prepare, she dipped and took him into her mouth. Her tongue ran over every inch, her teeth grazing lightly. She moved faster, sensing the tension build through his entire body, and then slowed to an agonizing pace where every inch she moved prolonged the torture.

Apparently, it was too much for him. With a growl, Nate grabbed Annie by her forearms and tugged her up to stand with him. His gaze penetrated her, his jaw locked in a hopeless attempt to keep control.

When Annie gave him a smug grin, he erased it with his mouth, searing her lips in a desperate kiss.

She was almost unable to breathe for the force of it. After a moment, she pulled away to catch her breath and watched the passionate fire blaze in his dark eyes. He didn't just want her. He wanted to possess her, consume her. Even after everything that had happened between them.

The weight of his desire was like an anvil pushing against her chest. Turning quickly in his arms, she pressed her bare back against him. In that moment, she needed to escape his intensity. It was almost frightening how much he wanted her. But even more so was how badly she wanted him. How much she craved not only the release, but the comfort and protection of being in his arms.

She'd always felt confined when she was held. It was never a comforting feeling for her but one that made her struggle for air. Nate's embrace had become like no other before. It was a safe haven from the world. It was...*home*.

Annie expected the panic to start welling in her chest, but it didn't. Which was even more disconcerting. She took a deep breath and eased back to let his firm arousal nestle against her rear. A quick sway of her hips brought a low hiss to her ear and was an easy distraction from her thoughts.

Nate's arms wrapped around her waist, tugging her back to sit in his lap as he plunged down into the spa. The buoyancy of the water made it easy for Annie to rise up and take all of him in with one quick thrust.

He groaned against her shoulder, holding her tight and still against him. After a moment, his hands glided across her skin to encircle her rib cage. They drifted higher until he cupped one breast in each palm. Annie's nipples ached, tightening against his fingertips as they brushed across the hardened peaks.

Annie leaned back against his chest, straddling his muscled thighs. Nate rested his chin on her shoulder and moved slowly beneath her. It was an easy, rolling motion. Neither too quick nor too slow, but building.

He played her like an instrument. It wasn't long before every muscle in Annie's aching body was tensed and primed for release. But even as Annie raced to her climax with Nate quick on her heels, she could feel the last of her barriers coming down. The last thread that held her back snapped when she no longer had the desire to hold it tight.

Annie didn't just desire Nate. She didn't just care about him or find comfort in him. She was in love with him. And it scared the living daylights out of her.

Nine

Annie's game ended late the next afternoon when she broke her table and there wasn't enough time to bother regrouping. That done, she had some free time to kill. It was too early for dinner, too late to get involved in anything else. Nate was probably prowling around the tables, trying to keep his distance and not distract her. Gabe would want her to talk to some people and try to dig up some more information. For that very reason, she opted to do the opposite and watch a couple of games still in progress.

Annie was surprised to find Tessa playing at a table three down from her own. She honestly hadn't expected her to still be in the tournament. There were five players at the table, including her sister. A quick glance showed that two didn't have long left to play. Their chips were quite low, especially in comparison to Tessa and another player, Paul Stein.

The crowd applauded as Tessa won the hand. Annie bit her lip, watching her sister scoop the chips and restack them in front of her. She was doing extremely well, even against a former champion like Paul. That alone should've been her clue to turn and walk away. But she didn't.

A few hands went by without much fanfare. Tessa and Paul went back and forth taking the pot until one of the other players went out. Then Annie noticed something odd. Tessa was fidgeting.

One of the first things Annie had taught her sister was not to fidget at the poker table. But she watched as her sister looked at her cards and started twisting a ring on her finger. One of the other players across the table folded his hand despite having quite a bit of money in the pot. Paul and the other player were both oblivious and focused on their game.

Fidgeting was not uncommon at the poker table because they sat for so long. But even then, something about Tessa's movements seemed odd and deliberate. In the next hand, Tessa absentmindedly twirled a strand of hair around her finger. Only Annie would know it was something Tessa didn't usually do. The other man raised, driving up the pot, then lost moments later, giving her sister a big boost in chips.

Maybe it was more obvious because Annie knew her sister and her tics, but Tessa and the other player were working together. She hadn't spent much time with Tessa over the years, but childhood habits died hard. Every move she made felt deliberate or forced. Most people didn't worry about partners working together at a tournament because the table assignments were random. You'd have to have someone on the inside to ensure you were placed together, and that was nearly impossible to do.

Annie's throat started to close on her as surely as if she'd been stung by a bee. The flop went down and Tessa bet conservatively. The way you would if you were trying to lure other players into putting more money into the pot. At the moment, Paul was contemplating his bet. Every eye in the room was on him, even those of the security guard who was supposed to be watching Tessa play.

All except for Annie's. Her gaze stayed glued on her sister as Tessa watched the other players and once again started curling a red strand of hair around her finger. It played out just as before, with her partner betting high. Tessa casually looked up and caught Annie watching her with a sad, disappointed expression.

Tessa froze for a moment in panic before smiling uneasily. She knew Annie had caught her but was confident her protective older sister was no threat to her scheme. She silently pleaded for Annie's silence, mouthing the word *please* before turning back to her hand.

Suddenly the last gap in her throat closed and Annie couldn't breathe.

From the moment she'd seen Tessa and Eddie together, this had been her secret fear. She'd been telling Nate the truth when she said she didn't know anything. Worrying about her sister's judgment and knowing for certain of her guilt were two very different things. Everything had just changed. She needed to get out of there. Now.

Without staying to see how the hand ended, Annie turned on her heel and began pushing her way through the crowd. She had no idea who was around her or who she knocked into on her way. All she knew was the panic and struggle for air. Her chest felt heavy, as though bricks were threatening to crush her rib cage.

She glanced at the entrance to the casino, but that wasn't enough. She needed clean air. Air without taxicab smog, tourists and the deafening bustle of the Vegas Strip.

Annie wanted to go to the roof.

Nate's private elevator didn't go all the way to the hotel roof, but she knew which one did. Her access card would take her almost to the top, and then she could scale the last few stairs.

"Annie?"

Someone called her name, but she couldn't stop to find out who it was. She darted down the hallway and into the secured area. The elevator was waiting when she arrived, and she slipped in her card to take her all the way to the top.

"Annie? Wait!"

It was Nate, she could tell now with the casino noises muffled by the doors. The voice was more urgent, his pounding footsteps echoing on the tile floor as he chased after her, but she ignored him. She needed to get away from everything, including Nate.

The doors closed and the car shot up from the ground floor at a dizzying speed. Annie closed her eyes. She was relieved to find the higher she climbed, the easier she could breathe. By the time she opened the door that led out to the roof, she felt infinitely better.

Annie took a deep breath and walked out onto the open expanse of the hotel roof. Her trembling hands gripped the railing as she stood, overlooking the twinkling lights of the Strip. The sun had already set, and the casino signs were growing more intense as the golden light faded from the sky.

She stood quietly listening to her surroundings, waiting for her heart to grow steadier in her chest. She strained to hear the deep boom of what could only be the Treasure Island cannons as the pirates battled out front.

She'd failed Tessa. If she'd been the sister she should've been, Tessa wouldn't have fallen into this sort of situation, letting herself be manipulated by a man. And after all the grief her sister had given Annie over her marriage! Marrying Nate wouldn't land her in jail.

What could she do now? Nate desperately wanted to secure the tournament contract. She had no doubt he would have Tessa arrested once he had enough evidence, and she'd told him she would turn the information over if she found it. The key was that she wouldn't look for her sister's guilt, but she'd just been slapped in the face with it.

How could she choose between her sister and the man that she loved?

She never should've come back to the Desert Sapphire. The tournament wasn't worth it. Not even the divorce was worth it. Nothing justified the pain and drama that coming back had brought. In the end, everyone would get hurt, including Nate. She'd promised herself she wouldn't hurt him again.

Alone in the rapidly deepening darkness, Annie let the last of the barriers go. The tears rushed down her cheeks in earnest, the first real tears she'd cried in years. Salty streaks ran down her flushed cheeks like a faucet had been turned on. She could only hold on to the wall for support as her body was racked with her emotional outburst.

When the sobs subsided and her face was impossibly red and swollen from her tears, she had to admit she felt better. Nothing had changed, but letting off the steam did wonders for her general outlook.

"Annie?"

At least she *was* feeling better. Nate's voice called to her from across the roof, but she didn't turn. Couldn't turn. She didn't want him to see her like this.

Nate's warm hand rested on her shoulder. His firm fingertips pressed soft circles into her tensed muscles. "Are you okay?"

Annie nodded, afraid to speak out loud and give away her lie.

"Tell the truth, Annie. What's the matter?"

"It's nothing." She sniffed, wiping at her cheeks in a dismissive way before turning to him. "Really."

"You are a terrible liar, Mrs. Reed."

Annie's stomach sank with the way he said those words. His voice had so much concern and emotion in it that her chest tightened. She'd never had that with anyone else. Her mother didn't tolerate weakness, and she had never really been outwardly affectionate. She loved her daughters, but sometimes it was hard to know it. Annie had learned early to keep her emotions on the inside. When she got older, poker seemed like the perfect career choice. But after years of holding it in, she didn't know how to let it out and truly open up to Nate.

He slipped a hand under her chin and gently turned her face up to look at him. She couldn't avoid eye contact now. The dark brown depths of his eyes pulled her into the comfortable warmth they offered. Standing there, she was almost able to forget the horrible mess she'd gotten into. At least until his hand glided around to her back and flipped the switch, turning off the recording device. At least he'd remembered before she lost her senses and started confessing to him while Gabe listened to every word.

"Do you need to get out of the hotel for a while?"

Annie's gaze narrowed at his words. She expected him to sense her weakness and pounce on it, but he didn't. Instead, he offered her an out and she would gratefully accept it. She wasn't ready to admit she'd seen Tessa cheat with her own two eyes. Or to confess she was in love with him and scared to death that she would lose him in all this.

He accepted her silence as a yes and pulled her into his arms. Annie accepted his embrace, collapsing onto him. She buried her face in his chest, drying her tears and keeping her from saying the words on the tip of her tongue. That he was right to be suspicious of her and of Tessa. That she was torn between protecting her sister and losing the man she loved.

"I've booked dinner reservations for us at the Eiffel Tower restaurant tonight." Nate took her hand and pressed a soft kiss on her fingertip. The loving gesture sent a warm surge through her that she wasn't expecting. She was distraught, emotionally spent, and yet she still wanted him. She craved not only the sensations he coaxed, but the safety and comfort she found in his arms.

He planted a kiss to the palm of her hand, then her wrist, working his way up to tickle the inside of her elbow and nip the soft skin of her upper arm.

The effect was immediate and powerful. Annie pushed everything out of her mind and let her body take over. She leaned into him, arching her back to expose her neck as he moved higher. If she was about to lose everything, she was going to indulge in every minute she had with him and savor each touch as her last.

Nate curved an arm around her waist, tugging her tight against him as his lips danced across her skin.

"Nate?"

"Yes?" he breathed against her ear.

"What time are our dinner reservations?"

"Not for another two hours."

"Good. Take me to the suite."

Nate arranged for the hotel limo to pick them up and whisk them down the Strip for dinner reservations at the Paris Hotel. Their table at the Eiffel Tower restaurant had premium views of the Bellagio fountains across the street. It was a breathtakingly romantic setting, even more so than Carolina's, she dared say.

He'd preordered the eight-course tasting menu with all the chef's specialties, substituting the first course because he knew Annie didn't care for caviar. As always, she was taken aback by Nate's ability to remember the details and make someone feel special. It was a powerful aphrodisiac to have someone that focused on her needs and desires both in and out of the bedroom.

"You're such a charmer," she said, sipping sparkling water from a crystal flute. "Hard for a woman to resist when you're in full-on Nate mode."

"What is that, exactly?" He looked at her quizzically. Apparently no one had ever pointed it out to him before.

"When you focus on someone. You make sure every detail is perfect, that they have everything they could possibly desire. It's an intense feeling."

"Did the other men in your life not treat you like the jewel you are?"

Annie chuckled softly. "Most men don't, actually."

He seemed surprised. "Then they're fools."

"Tell me the truth," she said, leaning across their second-course plates. "Are you like this with all women?"

Nate's smile dimmed almost imperceptibly. "No. Just you."

Annie swallowed her bite of food with difficulty, taking a large sip of water to try to force it down. She'd always told herself that Nate's charm was part of a savvy business strategy, that he treated her just as well as he did any customer. Knowing that was not the case was exciting and unnerving.

Their situation was complicated, to say the least. They were sharing a bed, knowing they were days away from divorce if all went according to plan. And yet now, sitting in this beautiful restaurant and feeling her heart swell every time he smiled, she knew things had changed. The thought of walking away from Nate in just a few days' time was almost painful.

But regardless of how she felt, divorce was still the smart choice. They wanted different things. That didn't mean her heart understood. It only knew what it wanted, and that was Nate. She'd been denying her feelings for so long it had become second nature. But she didn't want to suppress it anymore. She wanted to tell him that she loved him.

A shudder ran down her spine that she covered by slipping back into her sweater under the pretense of being cold. Just thinking the word *love* had given her chills. Saying it out loud seemed impossible. Especially with how things stood with Tessa. As much as her heart wanted to be free, it also needed to be protected. She couldn't trust Nate with it yet. Could she?

The dinner continued with relaxed, casual conversation. They enjoyed every bite of their food, paying their bill in time to walk downstairs and experience the fountains in person.

They stood at the railing along the dark pool, Nate's arm wrapped around her waist to hold her tight against him and keep her warm in the cooling desert air. "You'll love this," he whispered into her ear, planting a warm, affectionate kiss on her cheek. She'd told him she'd never seen the show, so he insisted they watch it here instead of from the restaurant.

She still fought the urge to tell him. There, with the swell of the music and the water dancing so elegantly among the colored lights, it seemed like the most natural thing in the world to say she loved him. That she always had. She needed to confess why she'd run and that she'd regretted it every day of the past three years. It was the right moment.

The music thundered the finale and, at last, the lights dimmed and the water went still. The crowds of people around them dispersed, but they stayed at the railing.

"Did you like it?" he asked.

"Yes, it was wonderful." And it was. But not nearly as wonderful as it was to watch it with him. How many other things in her life would be better because he was a part of it? If she didn't speak up now, she might never know. She wished she hadn't seen Tessa play today. Perhaps then she would have the confidence to speak her heart's desires without the fear of her sister's deception ruining it all. And it still might. But maybe if she told him how she really felt before any of it came to light, he would know she meant it. And they might survive it.

Annie turned to look at Nate. His dark eyes watched her face, a finger reaching out to gently move a strand of hair back behind her ear. It was those little things, those intimate gestures that convinced her he cared, even if he hadn't said it. It gave her confidence to finally speak.

"Nate?" she said, her voice nearly a whisper.

"Yes?" he said.

She'd spoken before her brain could talk her out of it, but now she wasn't certain what she should say. "I…I want to stay." She stumbled through her words.

"Stay? At the fountains?"

"No," she said, taking a deep breath. "I want to stay with you…beyond the tournament."

Nate's eyes widened with surprise, but he remained silent, almost as though he wasn't quite sure he could trust his ears.

"These last few days have been wonderful. I'm not

ready to give that up yet. If you're willing, I'd like to give us another try. A real try. Because…" Her heart stopped in her chest, the confession of love still lingering on the tip of her tongue. "I think I've fallen in love with you."

Nate swallowed, the lines of his throat working hard as he struggled with a response. She could see the conflict in his dark eyes. The hurt from before was still on his mind, and there was no way she could erase that from his memory. She could only replace it with new, better memories.

She turned away, looking down at the dark, swirling water. His silence pressured her to speak and fill the void. Somehow it was easier to confess in the dark when she didn't have to look at him. "If you aren't interested, I understand. I mean, I know this isn't what this week was supposed to be about. I know that you have no reason to forgive me for what I did to you. But I've always loved you. Even then. It just scared the hell out of me. It was such an intense feeling I couldn't take it. But being away from you was worse. I'd learned to live with the pain, but coming back here made it impossible. I don't want to leave again."

"Then don't," was his quiet reply. His fingertips pressed into her, pulling her closer. "Stay with me."

Annie closed her eyes and leaned into him. Her head rested against his shoulder. It wasn't a declaration of love, but it wasn't a rejection.

There was still hope that, in time, there would be more.

Ten

Nate couldn't sleep. He woke up just before dawn and found his brain whirring a hundred miles an hour. Something was bothering him, but he couldn't quite put his finger on what it was. He should be happy. Annie wanted to stay with him. She'd confessed she was in love with him. And yet…he hadn't quite let himself fully believe her words. She had said those things before and she'd left. What would make it different this time?

He rolled over in bed and looked at Annie in the dim light. She was curled into a ball beside him, her soft breathing the only sound in their room. Watching her sleep was always one of his favorite things. But he was too wound up to just sit there.

He quietly flung back the sheets, tugged on some lounging pants and made his way down the hallway to his office. He switched on the small lamp. It illuminated his corner of the room and revealed the blue personnel file sitting on his desk.

Darrell Thomas.

Nate had too many employees to know the names of every single one, but it frustrated him that he couldn't immediately put his finger on who this guy was. He reached out and flipped open the file. A color print of his badge photo and a copy of his sheriff's card were attached to the front.

He didn't recognize him. Darrell was fairly nonde-script. He was slightly heavyset with short dark hair and a closely cropped beard. None of his features were particularly noteworthy. He was the kind of person you saw and immediately forgot. It probably suited him well, given his line of work.

Darrell had a clean record. You couldn't get a sheriff's card without one. They usually did a thorough screening before they hired someone, but if he was good enough not to get caught, there was nothing to stop them. He found several positive performance reviews. Good, solid work references. He had ten years of experience as a dealer in Vegas, with the past two at the Sapphire. He'd also worked at a couple downtown casinos and the Tangiers before coming here.

Nate's jaw clenched as it occurred to him how many opportunities this man had had to cheat not only him, but also other players, over the years. People like him had nearly destroyed this hotel when Nate was a teenager. His father had sat back, powerless to stop the vultures that pecked at the broken carcass of his life. Nate was not vulnerable like his father. Tournament contract or not, he wouldn't tolerate this in his hotel.

He glanced at his desk clock. Gabe was as poor a sleeper as he was. They both worked ridiculous hours and drank far too much coffee. Nate grabbed his radio and put out a call to his head of security. "You around, Gabe?"

"Yep. I've actually been here all night, running through those videos from yesterday afternoon. You may want to come down here. It's some interesting tape."

Nate frowned. He'd made a quick call to Gabe before

dinner while Annie was in the shower. He'd asked him to find video of Annie in the casino yesterday afternoon. He'd never seen her that upset. She wasn't the kind of woman who was easily rattled and wasn't really forthcoming with her feelings. Finding her on the roof, hysterical and sobbing, had him worried. Something had gotten to her. Something she didn't want to tell him.

Nate needed to see what had set her off and hoped that there would be a video clip of it. Nearly every square inch of the casino was monitored with surveillance cameras, so he was certain it was on film. It was just a matter of locating Annie in thousands of hours of digital recordings.

"I'll be right down." Nate dressed quickly and headed downstairs to the security offices. He found Gabe facing a panel of surveillance screens, cuing up a clip of tape date-stamped the day before. "What did you get?" he asked, leaning over Gabe's shoulder.

"Well, it took me a while, but as you know, I have no life. I was able to narrow down the tapes based on where you saw her last and the time. Although I do have to warn you, I ended up finding more than you probably bargained for."

A sinking feeling settled in Nate's stomach as the gray screen unscrambled and began to play.

"You said you saw her take off around this time, so I'm cuing up the video a couple minutes before." Gabe tapped a finger against a woman's image on the screen. "You can see her here, walking through the casino."

Nate watched as Annie moved through the crowd, stopping to watch another table still in play. She looked interested, nodding and clapping appropriately as hands were won. "What table is she watching there?"

"Five."

Nate flipped open his file and started looking at yesterday's play statistics. The winner of table five had been Tessa Baracas. She'd outplayed quite a few big names. "Tessa beat Paul Stein?"

"I know. It would take a miracle for her to beat out a former champion. Or maybe just a little help. Check out the name of the dealer."

Nate's gaze ran over the sheet, and what he saw forced a muffled curse. "Darrell Thomas. I know we let him keep dealing so we could catch him in the act and not tip off the others, but please tell me you got him for something."

"Darrell hasn't taken a leak without a security shadow since we caught wind of his involvement, but even then we've got almost no evidence to charge him. I keep letting him deal in the hopes we'll have a break. Whatever they're doing, they're good. Watch this."

Nate looked up to watch the video again as Annie's passive expression changed. Her face stiffened, her eyes visibly widening despite the poor video quality. Her head shook subtly from side to side as she looked at someone off camera. Then she started to hyperventilate. Her hand flew to her chest as she spun and disappeared from the frame.

"Wow." Whatever she'd seen at that moment had not only been bad, but unexpected. And yet she hadn't run to him with the news, either.

"That's what I said. She didn't like what she saw. Made me curious, so I kept digging." Gabe fiddled with the digital files, bringing up a clip from another camera. "This one was from the overhead camera on table five." His finger brushed over the tops of the remaining players' heads. "We've got Paul here, Tessa here and then Darrell Thomas dealing, of course."

They watched in silence, trying to detect what happened, but it was hard to see. Darrell dealt her cards. She looked at them, pulling them toward her, and then sat fidgeting with her hair. That had to be when it happened, but if they'd cheated in that moment, it would be hard to prove in court with a video like this.

"Run it back again." The recording ran a second time, but there was still nothing to see. Nate's frustration was mounting. There had to be something. A slight detail he was missing. Something, anything, to nail them with.

"Wait, watch this next part," Gabe encouraged.

Nate narrowed his eyes at the screen as Tessa looked up from her cards and gazed into the crowd. From the angle, they couldn't see her face, but after a moment, she turned back to her cards and continued to play.

"I think Annie saw it happen. Whatever they did." Gabe cued up the tapes to the exact same time on two adjacent screens and paused them. "It's hard to tell, but Tessa is looking in the direction where Annie is standing. Right after that, Annie shakes her head. Perhaps they had some sort of private exchange that panicked Annie and sent her running."

"Damn." Nate flopped back into a chair and clapped his hands to his thighs. He felt as if he'd been punched in the gut. "No wonder she was upset. She knows she has the proof we need."

This was exactly what Nate had been worrying about. Why he'd kept his feelings for Annie to himself even as she looked at him and silently pleaded for him to respond in kind to her declaration of love. There was something about it that hadn't rung true.

He wanted to trust Annie. He wanted to believe her when she said she didn't have any knowledge of Tessa's involvement. He wanted her confession of love and offer to stay beyond the tournament to be more than just a ploy to protect her sister.

But he was a cynical, practical businessman and knew better. If a person felt the noose tightening on them, they would say or do anything to save themselves. Or someone they loved. The truth of the matter was that Annie had come to Vegas to play poker and get a divorce, not for a reconciliation. Her offer might be nothing more than a bargaining attempt.

Or perhaps she really did mean it and was conflicted about her knowledge.

Either way, when the tournament was over, Nate was fairly certain he would lose Annie no matter what was said or done.

Hell, he wasn't certain if he'd ever had her back in the first place. He had no real way of knowing if Annie cared about him or anything but her tournament. But, damn it, *he* cared. He didn't want to choose his life's work over Annie. How dare she put him in a position where he had to choose between doing the right thing and losing out on their chance at happiness together?

Gabe's voice startled him out of his thoughts. "It gets worse. Look at your schedule for today."

He flipped open the file, grabbing the page. It was easy to find Annie's name among the rapidly dwindling roster. She was playing on table six today. His finger ran over the list, pausing at the other names there. So was Tessa. "How the hell did they end up at the same table? That's against tournament regulations. Patricia wouldn't do that. She knows better."

"Yes, like you said, someone is tampering with the schedule. Normally someone would complain, but they've both been doing so well, the other players might be happy to see one knocked out. This could be a positive development," Gabe reasoned. "At this point, we don't have enough evidence to get Tessa or Darrell, and even Keith Frye's testimony won't get us much unless we can use it to pressure one of them to confess. We need more time, and only one person in that group is going to make it through to the final table tomorrow. If you could get Annie to let Tessa win, we c—"

"Impossible," Nate interrupted. There was no sense in letting Gabe go on. "She'd never go along with that. This tournament is everything to her."

Gabe sighed. "Okay, well, how about getting her to help us expose them somehow? If she saw what happened yesterday, she knows how they work. She tells us, we watch closer. Maybe we can catch them in the act. Or if she sees them do it again, she can tip us off. Give us some sort of signal."

"That's a lot of *if*s, Gabe."

The security manager frowned. "You don't think she'd do it? She wants to win, doesn't she? If Tessa is cheating, it's possible that Annie might not make it to the next round. I don't know about you, but that would irritate me, even if it was my sister."

Nate nodded. He was right. If given the choice, Annie would choose the tournament.

Gabe said something else, but Nate didn't hear him. His mind was deeply entrenched in the best way to approach Annie. It was a delicate subject. No one liked cheaters, but it was even worse in their culture to be a snitch. They'd gone to a hell of a lot of trouble to keep her spying a secret, not that he'd minded, but now that it involved Tessa, he had no leverage.

If she wouldn't help him voluntarily, he'd have to set aside their personal relationship and play this game as he would with anyone else.

* * *

Annie made it to the tournament area that morning without seeing Nate or Tessa. To tell the truth, she was relieved. She needed to focus on her game, and seeing either of them would just remind her of the rock and hard place she was wedged between.

She checked in and was assigned to table six. Only a few tables were left, with the top nine players advancing to the final table. If she won today, Annie would have made it further than she had in any tournament. She'd be guaranteed a handsome payout even if she went out on the first hand.

Even with everything going on, she couldn't help but grin with excitement as her game chips were reissued and she made her way across the loudly colored casino carpeting to begin the game. It was enough to make a girl's heart flutter with nerves, like kissing her first crush.

Only two other players were sitting at her table when she arrived. She recognized them both by face but couldn't remember their names. They were good to have made it this far, but their streak would end. Annie would see to it.

She found her assigned chair at the table and settled in. There were still a few minutes before game time, so she closed her eyes and tried to gather her focus.

"Annie, may I speak with you privately for a minute?" Nate's voice came over her shoulder, but it was unusually stiff and formal. She told herself it was because of the tournament. They were publicly a couple, but he was always professional.

Still, she frowned, getting up slowly from the table. "What's the matter?" she asked. Was her wire malfunctioning again?

Nate caught her elbow and led her a good distance

from the tournament area. "There's a problem," he said once out of earshot. His face was gravely serious, without the slightest hint of the man she'd made love to beneath it. "It's about Tessa."

Annie froze, her desire to return to the game table dwindling rapidly. He knew. She hadn't told him, but somehow he'd found out. She looked into his dark eyes, searching for a hint of how much information he really had. Her face tightened, her defenses rising to prevent her from giving away anything he could use against Tessa. "What about her?"

"I've seen the surveillance tapes from yesterday. I know you saw her."

Her eyes widened with panic. "Nate, I—"

He held up his hand to stop her. "Don't bother explaining. It isn't important."

"Okay," she said slowly. This was not the reaction she was expecting. She would actually be less disconcerted if he was angry and yelling. That, she expected. "So what do you want?"

"I wanted to warn you that Tessa is going to be playing at your table today."

Annie groaned before she could stop herself. It was bad enough playing against her sister, given how badly they both wanted to win. Knowing Tessa was cheating and could possibly bump Annie out of the tournament was even worse. "How could that happen?"

"Someone is manipulating the roster. But this is our chance to nail them. Tell me how they're doing it. We need to know if we're going to catch them at it."

Her throat went bone-dry in an instant. "No."

"Annie," Nate pressed, his voice calm and cold. "It's already too late to save her."

Her eyes widened as she frantically searched his face

for a sign he was bluffing in the hopes she would reveal the critical information he lacked. His jaw was firmly set, his dark eyes hurt that she hadn't been honest with him. But there were no signs of a bluff. He meant every word.

What choice did he leave her with? Either betray her sister or destroy her career. She tried not to let the disappointment creep into her voice. It ended up coming out in a hushed whisper. "I didn't know anything until yesterday."

"What did you see?" he pressed.

Tessa had dug a hole deep enough to bury them both. Annie might as well jump in. "I saw her signaling to another player. Watch her every gesture. Each move is deliberate. Whoever her partner is today will drive up the pot to help her win."

He nodded, his grip tightening on her elbow. "We're going to need your help to catch them."

At this, Annie closed her eyes. "Don't ask that of me, Nate. I can't do it. Even if it means putting Eddie in jail where he belongs."

"Annie, please." Nate's voice softened as he tried a new persuasive angle. "We need more evidence to build a solid case against Eddie."

And was she supposed to provide the evidence they needed? Not when it would do nothing but incriminate her sister and let Eddie walk away as he always did. Annie crossed her arms defensively over her chest, trying to rebuild some of the barricade that she'd let down between the two of them. She loved Nate, but she had to protect herself. "No. I told you what I saw. Your security people will have to do the dirty work."

At that, she reached under her sweater and ripped the wire from her skin without a thought about the pain. She shoved it into Nate's hands. "I have to go." She spun on her heels and rushed back to the table before she changed her mind and did something she would regret.

She came to a halt several yards from the tournament area to gather her composure. She closed her eyes and took a deep breath. Her hands smoothed over her hair and sweater, tugging at her skirt. By the time she took her third deep breath and opened her eyes, her furious heartbeat had slowed in her chest and she felt fairly in control.

Annie settled in her seat just as the announcement was made that the tournament was beginning. Tessa was sitting two seats to her right, but she didn't look at her sister. She didn't greet the other players or chat with the dealer. She also didn't look around for Nate or the navy-clad security officers who swarmed around the tables like sharks. Whether or not she'd wanted to cooperate, her role in Nate's plot was over and at last she only had to focus on the cards.

Make that the cards and the sharp ache in her chest. Her fit just now might have cost her the second chance with Nate she'd wanted, and in the end, it probably wouldn't change anything. Her sister was going to jail. The only thing she could do was focus on the tournament.

They were over an hour and a half into playing before Annie finally started to feel at ease. She was doing well. She'd won several key hands and at least one player was on the verge of going out. Tessa was playing a solid game, winning a few hands, but nothing suspicious. Today, her sister's earrings seemed to be secure and she wasn't fidgeting much. Not that she was looking.

After successfully winning a big pot, Annie drove the first player from the table. She stood to shake his hand and caught a glimpse of Nate over his shoulder. He was watching her, as he had all week, but this time he was not beaming with pride. He was scrutinizing her every move, his arms crossed over his chest, threatening to rip the shoulders out of his expensive black suit.

She didn't keep his gaze, sitting quickly and returning to the next hand. Annie needed to hold her game together. She couldn't let thoughts of Nate throw her off. She flipped up the corners of her new cards and frowned. The cards were good, she had no reason to frown, but she just couldn't shake the sensation of his eyes on her. How was she supposed to play with—

"Mrs. Reed?"

Her head snapped up at the sound of the dealer's voice. All the players were looking at her, including Tessa. "I'm sorry," she said, tossing a few chips out.

Focus, woman.

And she did. The next hour flew by in a blur of cards. The afternoon break came just as she began getting mentally weary. Annie stretched her legs, pacing around and avoiding anyone who looked as though they might want to talk to her.

The question plaguing her was what she would do next. Tessa was doing okay—not fabulous, but she wasn't the closest to going out, either. Annie hadn't specifically targeted her to knock out of the tournament, but maybe she should. The less time Tessa played, the less time Nate and his gorillas would have to gather incriminating information.

The call went out to summon the players to the tables so the next portion of the game could begin. With a sigh, Annie chucked her plate into the trash and made her way back. A quick scan around the crowd made her instantly suspicious. Nate and Gabe were gone.

Annie leaned back in her chair and eyed the black dome on the ceiling above them. No doubt they were watching from the office. At least now she couldn't spy

Nate scowling at her from across the room. Some of the pressure was gone, even if the gravity of her situation still sat heavily on her shoulders.

As the game resumed, Annie glanced quickly at the stack of chips in front of her sister. It would take a couple hands to wipe her out, but it could be done. Especially if Tessa was certain she had a sure thing.

Which she very well might have. Annie eyed the dealer. She hadn't played at any of his tables before. There was also a man playing at her table who she didn't know. He could be helping Tessa, but she wasn't sure.

Several hands went by without much progress. Annie would win, then Tessa would win, scissoring back and forth. Before long, there were just four of them left. If Annie was going to take out Tessa, she needed to do it, and soon.

The dealer began the hand and Annie had a queen and a jack of hearts in the hole. She bet accordingly. The flop went down containing the ten of hearts, the nine of clubs and the king of hearts.

Annie had a straight and she was one card away from a *very* good hand. The nine or ace of hearts would give her a straight flush or a royal flush. But it was nearly impossible to get and too soon to get excited.

Tessa bet a fairly large amount. It was too early for that, but Annie didn't react. She probably had a pocket pair to go with the flop. The bet was still too large just for three of a kind. If Annie raised her, Tessa would have to go all in. She considered her options and chose to raise. The other player folded.

Tessa didn't hesitate, pushing all her chips out and going all in. Annie felt her jaw tightening. She kept forgetting that her sister was cheating. If she was going all in, she knew something Annie didn't. Perhaps she anticipated more. Maybe four of a kind.

If Tessa had four of a kind, the only hands that would beat her would be the straight flush or royal flush. Annie was one impossible card away from an unbeatable hand. She had enough money to match Tessa's bet without going all in. She could take the risk and still be safe. If she folded, Tessa would win, anyway.

Annie took a deep breath and called, pushing her chips out. They both turned over their cards. She'd been right. Tessa had a pair of tens. Her sister looked at her, the smug satisfaction paling slightly when she saw Annie's hand. She'd thought she had a sure thing. Now, she wasn't certain. She could read Tessa's face like a book.

As she anticipated, the turn was a ten of spades. Annie sighed to herself, staring off into the crowd as she mentally calculated the odds of the river card being the nine or ace of hearts. It was astronomical. Having one in the same hand as someone with a four of a kind made it damn near impossible. Well, at least when one of the parties wasn't cheating.

The murmur of speculation ran through the crowd as everyone saw the cards and came to the same realization. Everyone knew the hand would be determined by the river card. An almost unbeatable hand was about to be tested in a glorious fashion. The kind of moment that video montages of poker tournaments would play for years to come.

Annie closed her eyes and held her breath. That was all she could do.

"What the hell is she doing?" Nate cursed and pushed his rolling chair back from the panel of screens. "She's deliberately trying to take Tessa out of the game."

He shouldn't be surprised. She was doing what she had to do to protect her sister and her own stakes in the game. He'd given her no choice. Tessa might not like it, but if she had any idea what Annie had just done for her, she wouldn't complain.

"Whoa." Gabe shook his head. "That's a helluva hand they've both got. Might backfire on her."

Nate leaned in. If the last card was the nine or ace of hearts, Annie would win and Tessa would be out. He was a casino owner. The odds were miserably against her. And yet she was determined to take Tessa down. He stood and took a few paces away from the screen. He couldn't watch.

"Well, I'll be damned! The ace of hearts, man. Tessa is out."

"Damn!" He slammed his hand onto the console, making the screens flicker just slightly.

"We didn't get anything on her."

Nate sighed and shook his head. "Have security quietly escort Tessa upstairs. We didn't get anything conclusive, but she doesn't know that. She's young and inexperienced. With a little pressure, her mouth will start running like an old faucet."

Eleven

Annie knew better than to go up to the suite after the tournament was done for the day. There was a fight waiting for her there, she just knew it. Instead, she started wandering aimlessly through the casino. She wanted to get as far away from the poker tables and the cameras as she could. She turned down a narrow corridor, relishing the quiet and solitude. A placard on the wall indicated she would follow the route to get to the hotel gym and day spa.

Perhaps now was a good time for that manicure.

She turned to continue down the hall, then stopped when she found Jerry, the Sapphire's floor manager, standing in her path.

"Mrs. Reed," he said with a smile.

"Afternoon, Jerry," she said. "I'm off to get my nails done as a reward for another successful day of the tournament."

"Well, I'm sorry to interrupt your plans, Mrs. Reed, but I'm going to have to escort you upstairs."

Annie's blood froze instantly in her veins. Nate must be furious with her if he'd sent his casino manager to collect her. Her gaze dropped from Jerry's apologetic smile to the gun held close to his side. In an instant, she knew she no longer had the advantage in this hand.

"Jerry, I…" she started, taking a step back toward the chaos of the casino.

Jerry surged toward her, reaching out to grip her upper arm with his free hand. "It will be best for everyone involved if you come with me without making a scene."

Annie ignored the cruel fingers digging into her upper arm and nodded softly. He tugged her forward and she fell into step beside him. At first, she'd thought perhaps she was getting an inside view at the rougher side of casino security. But the farther they moved away from the part of the hotel where the surveillance and interviews took place, the more concerned she became. Casino managers didn't carry guns. And security would've taken her upstairs if she'd been implicated. Things had just gone unexpectedly awry.

Now it was too late. They walked the quiet, abandoned hallways, moving deeper into the bowels of the casino, away from the possibility that someone could help her or spot her on the security monitors that Nate was always watching. If she'd only kept that wire on instead of throwing it in his face…

They took one of the staircases up a few floors and into a hallway of guest rooms in one of the older segments of the hotel. Annie had never been into this part of the property. This portion was original to the casino Nate's grandfather had built. The shiny blue tower of fancy suites had been one of her husband's additions. These rooms here were nice, but you could feel the age, still smell the faint cigarette smoke from back before it was banned in most of the facilities.

Jerry didn't look at her as they walked, stopping only at the end of the hallway to open the door to one of the rooms. There was no room number, just a sign that designated the space as private.

He shoved her inside and to her surprise, it was less of a hotel room and more of an office space like Nate's quarters. There was a seating area with a television, a conference table with leather chairs and a desk piled high with paperwork.

"Where are we?" she asked.

"This used to be the suite where George Reed ran his casino. Any decisions were made in this very room. Nate, of course, wanted something a little flashier with his makeover, so he allowed me to use the space when I came back here to work for him."

"And why are we here?"

Before he could answer, Eddie Walker appeared through the doorway that led to living quarters of some kind. She was right. This had nothing to do with Nate. But everything to do with Tessa. It had never occurred to her that Nate wouldn't be the only one angry with her stunt today.

"Sit down, Annie." Eddie pointed to one of the seats surrounding a glass coffee table. When she hesitated, she felt the hard prod of the gun in her rib cage and it urged her forward.

She flopped into the chair, able at last to look at Jerry. She'd met him once over the past week but had never really given the man much notice. Nate had spoken of him a few times, grateful that a man with his experience was there to help him keep operations on track. She knew he'd worked with Nate's grandfather for years, then came back to work with Nate after an unfulfilling retirement, but that was it. No reason to suspect or ever consider Jerry had any reason to hold a gun on her.

"You played well today," he said, lowering himself

calmly into the opposite chair. "As always, I enjoy watching you. You're so much better than Tessa. Sometimes it's all we can do to keep her from putting herself out of the game, much less win."

Annie didn't know where they were going with this, but Jerry had the gun, so he could talk as long as he liked. He eyed her, the pistol now resting in his lap. She didn't doubt for a moment that the older man would spring to action with the gun if she even shifted in her seat.

"That, of course, is why I put you two at the same table today. With Nate and Gabe watching her every move, I knew you wouldn't let Tessa hang herself. Or interfere with you winning." He leaned back in his seat and chuckled. "That was quite a stunt you pulled off today. You're lucky my dealer was feeding you the cards you needed to beat her."

Annie let a ragged breath slip through her lips. The dealer helped her win? Suddenly, she realized her mistake. She'd thought she was doing the right thing, but she had played right into his plans. *She* was the one they were really after. They had just used Tessa to get to her.

"Tomorrow, the Barracuda is going to sweep the tournament," Jerry announced.

"Nate has probably arrested your dealer by now," she argued. "It won't work. They're watching everyone so closely."

"We have more dealers and another player heading to the final table tomorrow. They'll help us ensure that you'll win it all. After Tessa and Darrell are arrested, they'll relax their surveillance. No one will suspect you because they'll believe you were instrumental in catching the real cheaters. You'll be able to waltz out the door with your winnings."

Annie's heart started pounding frantically in her chest.

She had worked for years to win, but she wasn't a cheater. She couldn't. Wouldn't. "I don't want to win that way."

"You have no choice, Annie. Tessa going to jail could be the least of your worries. She was involved with some really dangerous people. Something might happen to her before her court date."

Annie swallowed hard and closed her eyes. She wouldn't let them hurt her sister. "My marriage will be ruined." She could barely imagine the expression on Nate's face if he found out she really was involved.

"From what I hear, your marriage was ruined the day you said your vows." He tapped the radio at his hip and sighed. "What's left of it will be destroyed tonight. You can't go back to the suite. I don't trust you not to tip Nate off."

"I won't, I—" she started, but he cut her off with a curt shake of his head.

"You're going to go to Nate and tell him it's over. That you've fulfilled your part of the bargain and now you want your own hotel room. After your stunt today, I doubt it will be a surprise. He'll be so distraught that tomorrow's outcome won't matter."

Annie's fists tightened in her lap, the anger coursing through her veins. Since she was old enough to make decisions, every facet of her life had been decided by her. Right or wrong, she was in charge of her fate. She'd left Nate before he could start telling her what to do. She certainly didn't want the likes of Eddie and Jerry calling the shots.

"What about him?" She jerked a thumb in the direction of Walker.

"He's leaving. They suspect him, so his disappearance will confirm they've caught the right people. It's all managed, Annie. I assure you that this is a well-organized plan. You'll walk away with the glory, a third of your winnings and most importantly, a guarantee of your sister's safety."

Somehow, winning the tournament paled in comparison to what it would cost her. She hadn't intended it to happen, but she had fallen in love with Nate. They had both grown up a lot since the last time they were together. They could have a future—one she'd never realized she wanted until she had Nate back in her life—but Jerry would force her to throw it all away.

And for what?

Even if she did everything she was told to do, there was no guarantee she could walk away from this. She would just be giving them more evidence to blackmail her into playing again. "And that's it?"

"Until such time that we see fit to call on your services again."

There it was. She was not just taking Tessa's place tomorrow; she was filling her shoes until Annie came under suspicion and they had to replace her. In the end, her career and her marriage would be ruined.

Despite his assurances, she would never be free of any of this. Tessa would never be safe. And Nate would never, ever forgive her.

Nate was having one of the longest days of his life. He'd kept telling himself that catching criminals and protecting his casino was the most important thing. After seeing Annie's reaction, he wasn't so sure. He hadn't had much time to think about it, though. Since Tessa was eliminated, he'd spent most of his evening in the security offices interviewing her and Darrell.

Hours of interrogation and working with the police had taken a lot of energy out of him. He wanted nothing more than to curl up in bed with Annie and sleep. Honest-to-God sleep, for more than four hours. Twelve would just about do it.

But he knew he was likely to get none of those things. He'd seen the look in Annie's eyes when he'd threatened her. He'd recognized the pain hidden there when he asked her to betray her sister and had forced her to choose. What choice did he have? He couldn't just let Tessa walk because she was his sister-in-law.

When the elevator chimed and the doors opened to his suite, he was surprised to find Annie sitting on the leather sofa in his office. The lights of the Strip shining through the picture window were the only thing illuminating her as she sat in the darkness waiting for him. She looked up when he came in, but there was barely a flicker of recognition in her eyes, much less a warm greeting.

Nate walked over into the mostly dark office, flipping on the lamp on his desk. The light was enough to highlight the tracks of tears that had dried on Annie's cheeks. His stomach immediately sank.

"How's my sister?" Annie spoke the words without looking at him. Her gaze was fixed firmly on her hands, folded in her lap.

"She's fine. A smart girl mixed up in something stupid. Hopefully they won't go too hard on her. She's working out a plea bargain with the D.A. for information to convict Darrell and Eddie."

"Just Darrell and Eddie?"

Nate frowned. Did she think he was going to have her charged, too? She should know better. Or should she? Hell, if she had been involved, Nate probably would've hauled her in, even if he regretted it later. "Yes. We don't have evidence of anyone else being involved at this point.

I think that's quite enough, to be honest. Tessa should be released on bail tomorrow morning."

"Good." Annie stood suddenly, scooping up her purse and grasping the handle of her rolling suitcase.

He didn't know why he was surprised. "Where are you going?"

She continued to hide beneath her dark lashes. Nate couldn't understand why she was hiding from him. What did she think he was going to see in her eyes?

"I'm going to check into my own hotel room. I think given the current situation it's the best idea."

"So you're leaving." It was more of a statement than a question, but Nate wanted to hear her say the words. When she left the last time, he hadn't been there. She'd written a note and slipped out in the night. If she was going to leave him again, he wasn't going to make it easy on her. It certainly wasn't easy on him.

"Yes, I'm leaving. I've fulfilled my end of the agreement. You've caught your bad guys. I don't see any need for us to continue with the charade."

Charade. It sure as hell hadn't felt like a charade. It had felt like she gave a damn. She'd confessed her love for him not twenty-four hours ago. Apparently it had all been smoke and mirrors to protect her sister. He couldn't keep the steely anger from his voice when he responded. "So I assume you're wanting me to keep my end of the deal and give you your precious divorce."

Annie took a deep breath, not answering right away. There was something in her hesitation that urged him to act. He was about to call her on it when her chin snapped up and her blue eyes fixed on him with unmatched intensity. "Yes. I still want the divorce."

Stupid. Nate was stupid. Even now, when faced with the truth about their relationship, he kept looking for reasons to believe in her. He'd started out this journey in the hopes of getting over Annie once and for all, but it had backfired. He'd ended up falling for her again. Gabe had been right about this whole thing being a bad idea. That fact pissed him off more than anything.

"So you're just going to run away again?" He stuffed his curled fists into his pockets to contain his anger.

"I am not running away!" A red flush rose to her cheeks and she crossed her arms tightly under her breasts. "I came here to play in the tournament and get a divorce. Just because you tried to twist this arrangement into something it wasn't doesn't mean I'm running away. I'm simply putting an end to this relationship once and for all."

Nate reached out to touch her arm and found her skin ice-cold. Her tell was giving her away. "Please don't lie to me, Annie."

"I never lied to you." Annie spoke the words, but the eye contact dropped and she turned to the window.

The frustration was starting to well up inside of him. How could she throw all this away? Again? He let his arm drop to his side. "You're lying right now. Acting like this week hasn't meant anything to you. Damn it, I think our relationship is more important than this situation with your sister. We can work this out."

"No, we can't. There's nothing to work out."

"Then you've changed your mind? You don't love me after all?"

"Nate, it doesn't mat—"

"Say it!" he interrupted, his voice booming loudly and reverberating off the walls of the small office. He hadn't meant to yell, but if that was the only way to get through to her, so be it. "If this whole thing is just a charade you went along with to get your prized freedom and protect your sister, then say it. I want to hear the words before you walk out on me again."

He expected her to get angry, to start yelling back at him. He wanted emotion out of her—any emotion. Instead, the expression on her face shifted in a way he almost couldn't see. She was struggling with something. Her feelings? Her loyalty to her family? Annie almost looked defeated, and he'd never seen that in her before. She was first and foremost a fighter.

Her eyes became glassy. She opened her mouth to speak two or three times before she finally found the words. "I…don't love you. I just said that because I thought I could talk you out of chasing Tessa."

Her statement rang with about as much truth as a politician's campaign speech. "I don't believe you." Nate stretched out a hand to her again, but she jerked back out of his reach.

She shook her head, blinking away tears she was too stubborn to shed. "It doesn't matter if you believe me. It doesn't matter if you love me. It's over, Nate. Goodbye."

Jerry better lock his bedroom door, or Annie would smother the old bastard in his sleep.

There were no words to describe how horrible it was to look into Nate's eyes and destroy their chance at happiness. Annie had managed to hold her tears back until the doors of the elevator closed, but she sobbed with abandon until she reached the casino floor.

Five seconds.

That's all it would've taken to tell him the truth, consequences be damned. To out Jerry for the rat he was. Instead, she'd done what she had to do to save her sister's life. At first, she hadn't been sure she could do it. When she said she didn't love him, he didn't believe her.

He saw through her bluff and wanted her, anyway. The redemption and love she'd found with him were everything she'd never known she needed. And she'd been forced to throw it all away.

Now she had nothing. Yes, she might walk away with the championship tomorrow, but there was no glory when she didn't earn it.

Defeated, she flopped down in front of a slot machine and stared blankly at the flashing lights of the screen that beckoned her to play. She wasn't interested. She preferred games of skill over games of chance. She liked having some control over her fate.

Her finger ran softly over the blinking buttons as she chuckled bitterly. Maybe she should give up poker for slots. She'd relinquished control in all the other areas of her life. Why not this, too?

"Ms. Baracas?"

Annie turned, surprised at being addressed by her maiden name for the first time in a week. Everyone in the hotel had been calling her Mrs. Reed. Apparently bad news traveled faster than the good.

It was a bellhop, dressed in the navy-and-gold uniform of the hotel. His name tag said his name was Ryan. "Mr. Reed requested that I bring you this." He held out one of the disposable room key cards. "Your new room is suite eleven fifty-three, up the west elevators near the keno lounge." With a quick, polite nod, he turned and vanished into the crowd.

Annie frowned and rotated the plastic key in her fingers. She should've known that Nate would think of everything. He always did. Even as upset as he'd appeared to be, he had managed to take care of all the loose ends. Her pride stung a bit for it. A part of her was hoping he'd be too distraught by her leaving, but what did she expect?

He'd managed to build a great hotel after she left the first time. Why would this be any different?

She was angry at him, although she had no right to be. She'd been the one to walk away. But it still hurt.

Annie stood up and headed toward her new room. She moved quickly, not wanting to run into anyone she knew right now. As it was, it felt as if every employee in blue was eyeballing her with contempt. Maybe it was just the guilt making her paranoid. She doubted a company-wide memo had been distributed in the last fifteen minutes.

As she reached the elevators, she was dismayed to find Jerry there, waiting for her. "I don't want to speak to you right now." Turning from him, she forcefully pressed the up button and crossed her arms over her chest.

He ignored her irritation and patted her on the shoulder in a paternal way that was completely alien to her. It was probably meant to be soothing and encouraging, but it wasn't. A real father wouldn't force her to do the things she'd done today.

"You're a good girl," he said before disappearing into the keno lounge.

Twelve

This was it.

Annie should be proud. This was the first time she'd ever made it to the final table of a main event. Unfortunately, what would've been a feather in her cap was tainted by what she was about to do today.

She sat down at the table, taking her assigned chair. As the others gathered, she pulled her compact from her purse and did a quick once-over of her makeup. The cameras and lights would be on her all day.

"You look like hell, kiddo." The Captain took his seat at the table, decked out in his favorite Hawaiian shirt. He always wore the blue one with the pink hyacinths at the final table. "Trouble in paradise?"

Annie tried to smile and dismiss his concerns, although she had to agree. The concealer did its best to cover the dark circles, but there was no hiding the drooping of her eyelids or the sleep-deprived fog that clouded her blue gaze. "I didn't sleep well last night. Just nervous about today, I think."

"Just focus on your game, Annie. Deal with the rest later."

They were wise words. She wished that she could,

but "the rest" had literally made its way into her game. She looked up at the Captain, a man who was probably as close to a father figure as she'd ever have. His blue-gray eyes saw straight through her in a way few people could. There was no way he could know what was really going on, but he had no trouble reading the strain etched into every inch of her body.

It probably wasn't hard, if she looked as bad as she felt. The granola bar and coffee she'd scarfed down were turning somersaults in her stomach. Her hands were shaking. She felt a sheen of nervous perspiration forming at her hairline and the nape of her neck. The needling sensation of anxiety was running up and down her spine. She was going to look like a nervous, sweaty, female version of Richard Nixon on national television, and that was the least of her problems.

"Thanks. Good luck, Captain."

He winked at her and Annie turned back to staring at her hands. For once, she wished she was one of the players who hid behind sunglasses and hats. Then maybe her vulnerabilities wouldn't show. Instead, she was on full display with her low-cut blouse and short skirt. She'd considered wearing jeans and a T-shirt today but felt the sudden change would alert the other players, and Jerry, to the fact that she was not at the top of her game this morning.

The Barracuda never showed weakness.

Annie closed her eyes to take a deep breath and center herself before the tournament started. When she did, Nate's face, pained with her betrayal, appeared in her mind just as it had last night every time she'd tried to sleep. Her eyes had popped open to avoid the disappointed expression of the man she loved, only to find the same look on his face across the room.

Nate was watching everything from a far corner. Not

her, per se, but overseeing the tournament. She'd expected he would watch from the security booth, but Jerry had been right. The bad guys were caught, the contract was secured and now the focus was on managing the VIPs and finishing up a successful tournament. What did they know?

His dark eyes ran across the room, stopping on her for just a fraction of a second. When their gazes met, there was a moment, an instant of connection. In that second, Annie saw the pain and confusion he was hiding behind his businessman facade. Then it was gone. He turned away to talk to one of his employees and Annie was once again alone in a room full of people.

The tournament started a few minutes later. The man seated to her far right was there to help her drive up the pots and win hands. Eddie had gone over all the signals with her. She didn't know his name, but she recognized him. Like her, he'd been specially "selected" to reach the final table without drawing suspicion. He smiled at her briefly before game play began. That would be the only recognition she'd get. The room was absolutely crawling with ESPN cameras. They had to be very careful.

Being stealthy was a whole new level of stress Annie wasn't used to when she was playing. She had to make subtle signals to the dealer and the other player so they knew what to do, all the while also focusing on winning.

The first few hours went well and without much help from the others. Two players were eliminated. She was so close to achieving her goal.

Then she spied Jerry and Nate talking to one another. Their discussion paused for a moment and both turned to watch her. Both gazes—that of the man she'd pushed away and the man who'd forced her to do it—were boring into her. The sensation was unnerving. It was as though her skin had been peeled back and she was thoroughly exposed. As though if he looked hard enough, Nate would see her for the poker cheat she'd always despised.

"Ms. Baracas?"

Annie's focus snapped back to the dealer. She wasn't paying attention at all. Making a quick assessment of what she'd missed, she tossed a few chips out and tried to regain her grip on the game. It didn't work. Despite the fidgeting and jewelry twirling, she lost a big hand. Then another.

It wasn't even lunchtime, but Annie could feel the tournament slipping away. It didn't matter what cards she was given or what else was going on at the table. She started losing. Not on purpose. She knew Jerry wouldn't stand for that and neither would her pride. And yet she watched her stack of chips dwindle away.

The remaining players could smell the blood in the water. She was short stacked and outnumbered. She folded her current hand to give herself time to think while the others played.

Annie was two big hands from being out of the tournament. Yes, she could still manage a dramatic comeback, but the odds were poor, even with help. The others would team up on her and drive her out of the game.

Easing back in her chair, Annie sighed. She was just prolonging her own demise and she knew it. So did Jerry.

She turned and caught his heated gaze from the left side of the table. He was alone, fuming and red faced as he watched. Apparently she was supposed to be doing better. Apparently she was going to be his big jackpot and meal ticket.

To hell with Jerry. To hell with him and this game, if dealing with the devil was her price for playing. He could hang his hopes on the other guy. It looked as though he would outplay her at this rate.

Annie scooted back up to the table with newfound enthusiasm. She was certain Jerry thought she'd been properly chastised for her performance and was ready to pick up her game. Hardly.

She took her cards. For a woman supposedly cheating, she had absolutely nothing. Not even a pair of threes or a face card. Running her fingers down the stack of her chips, she counted and raised, betting conservatively, as she would if she had a solid hand. She signaled to her partner that she had an excellent hand. He tossed in his chips while another folded. The pot grew, the flop went down. Annie still had nothing. She could see her friend and fellow player Eli out of the corner of her eye. He kept jiggling his sunglasses. That was his tell when he had good cards. Normally, she'd sit this hand out, especially with the crap she'd been dealt. Instead, she bet again. If this was the last hand of poker she ever played, she was going down in a blaze of glory.

The turn went down and as she hoped, she had the worst hand ever. She went all in. The remaining players folded. Eli called, they both revealed their hands and the river card was turned.

It was time to put an end to this.

Nate gave up watching the tournament early. Annie wasn't playing well, and his angry glare wasn't helping. Despite everything that had happened between them, he wanted her to succeed. So he'd gone to his office for a few hours.

On his desk, he found the courier's package from her lawyer that he'd fished out earlier. The first time it had arrived, he'd laughed and phoned his attorney to throw a monkey wrench into her plans. Now, he held it with a sense of somberness and finality.

There had been a fleeting moment this week when he'd thought he might not need this paperwork any longer. That night at the fountains when Annie had confessed to him, he'd had a glimmer of hope. Despite everything else going on, he'd started to believe that what really mattered—the two of them and how they felt about each other—might survive the rest. He'd held that tiny flame of possibility tight against his chest even as she told him she didn't love him and was just protecting Tessa.

But maybe he was just like a child who refused to believe the truth about Santa when he was faced with the cold, hard facts. He clung to the fantasy because he was certain Annie was lying. But why? There was no logic to her actions that he could find.

It might have just come down to being unable to stay with the man convicting her sister, no matter how much she cared. No matter how much he cared, although he'd never voiced his feelings to her the way he should've.

Nate flipped the cover page over to view the divorce paperwork. The settlement was simple—no assets to divide, no custody battles. They were each walking away with what they'd come into the marriage with, despite having no prenuptial agreement in place. Annie was technically entitled to half of what he had. She could take half of the hotel, force him to sell his home and raid his savings and retirement funds. It could be a huge hit to his finances. And yet, despite his stalling and aggravating her, all she'd wanted was her freedom.

So he'd give it to her.

Nate slipped the paperwork from the envelope and read over the divorce decree. It was amazing to him how one little slip of paper could dissolve not only a marriage, but all the promise and potential it had. Although he'd told her he'd refused to sign to force her here and make her suffer, he knew now that he hadn't been ready to give up on them yet. And he didn't want to give up now. He loved Annie. He always had—he was just too stubborn to admit it to himself before now.

But Nate knew it was time to let it go. Annie had made it perfectly clear that she was done. If he'd fallen for her again, that was his problem, not hers.

Pulling a pen from his coat pocket, Nate smoothed out the paperwork on the desk and signed his name on the dotted line. That done, he slipped the platinum wedding band from his finger and took a deep breath. It was as if a burden was taken off his shoulders. He'd carried this marriage on his own for far too long.

He slipped the papers back into the envelope and radioed someone to take it to Annie's suite. He didn't want the papers sitting near him any longer than they needed to be. He might be tempted to tear them up or run them through his shredder.

For a moment, Nate considered calling Gabe and seeing if he was up for a night on the town when the tournament was done. He couldn't remember the last time he'd gone out. His own hotel had a club frequented by the Hollywood elite where he could commandeer the VIP suite, gather a crowd of people and lose himself in the hedonism of the town he'd lived in his entire life. A couple drinks and a couple willing ladies might be just what he needed to put this mess behind him.

He eyed his cell phone and then with a sigh, Nate let reality creep back in. That was the last thing he needed. Instead, he pulled out some business papers and returned to the work of running his casino.

* * *

It was over. Finally.

She hadn't won, but that was fine with her because she didn't want to give Jerry the satisfaction of taking the tournament. Until today, she'd done well enough without his help, although now he was going to walk away with two-thirds of her winnings. It was a small price to pay if Tessa was safe. Perhaps he wouldn't bother either of them again if he thought Annie didn't have the chops to make it to the final table in another tournament.

She'd completed a couple interviews and gone through the motions of wrapping up her tournament. It was the typical process, but this time she couldn't bear it. The lights and the cameras and the questions were just too much for her to take. One reporter had even had the audacity to ask her about her marriage to Nate and if it had contributed to her choking today. It took everything she had to maintain composure and not take out her aggravation on the blonde.

She just wanted to get back to Miami. She had no idea what she would do once she got there, but anywhere was better than here.

She wasn't a fool, though. As badly as she wanted away, Annie asked casino security to escort her to her room and waited for someone to be available. She'd made that mistake once, but even Jerry wasn't dumb enough to pull a stunt with one of Gabe's guys with her. The guard saw her safely inside and waited until she'd securely bolted the lock and thanked him through the door.

Once inside, Annie headed straight to her bedroom to pack. If she was quick, she could catch a late-afternoon flight and get out of town before Nate or Jerry could come looking for her. Right now, she couldn't deal with either of them. Her only hope was that Tessa was smart enough to do the same once she made bail.

Annie grabbed her bag from the closet and swung it up onto the bed. It wasn't until then that she noticed the tan envelope lying on the comforter. Her name was written on it in Nate's neat penmanship.

She held the envelope in her hand for a moment before she could work up the nerve to open it. When her nail slipped under the flap, it popped open to reveal the familiar papers stapled to the blue binding of legal documents. Her gaze ran over the first few words of the page, her heart sinking deeper into her chest with each letter.

Decree of Divorce.

She jumped to the bottom of the page, where she found Nate's signature awaiting her own.

She'd expected to feel happy or at least relieved. This was what she'd wanted. What she'd practically sold her soul for. And yet tears immediately began welling in her eyes at the sight of his scrawled name.

Annie flopped onto the bed and let the papers slip from her fingers to the floor. This was what she'd thought she'd wanted for the past three years, but for once, achieving her goals didn't give her the adrenaline high she lived for. She felt awful. Her stomach ached with dread, her chest was tight with a pain she hadn't felt since…since she'd made herself walk away three years ago.

Then, she'd lied to herself and said she didn't really love him. Convinced herself that marriage was the terrible institution her mother had always ranted against. It had been enough then to propel her fast and far away from the temptation of Nathan Reed.

It took months, but eventually she'd believed it and the pain faded. At least until she lay in her cold, lonely bed and the truth crept in.

But Annie didn't want to lie anymore. Not to herself and not to Nate. She wanted to be with him. If that meant being married, she would be married. Their relationship was wonderful and special and she didn't want to throw it away again because of that bastard casino manager or her own irrational fears of commitment.

A knock sounded and she heard Nate call her name. Annie's heart soared as she raced to the door. This was her chance. She wanted to tell him everything. To confess her every sin and beg him to forgive her.

Flipping the locks as quickly as she could, Annie flung open the door. Nate was nowhere to be found. Instead, Eddie was there with a digital voice recorder in his hand. He hit the stop button with a smile.

She needed to run. To slam the door shut and call security. Her second of hesitation cost her the opportunity. She only had long enough to register the sharp pain to her head and the sudden blackness that followed.

Thirteen

Nate knocked twice without a response before he used his master key to open the door to Annie's suite. He shouldn't abuse his powers this way, but he frankly didn't care anymore. He needed to talk to her. He'd come back downstairs after she was eliminated, but she was nowhere to be found. She hadn't checked out of the hotel yet, so he'd come here.

He was discouraged to find the room mostly dark except for a light in the bedroom. There were no signs of life in the suite. "Annie?" he called out before approaching the bedroom door, easing it open with his hand. There was no answer.

The room was empty, the bed made. There was no luggage in the closet, no makeup on the bathroom counter. Annie was already gone.

Frustrated, he turned and headed back through the room, pausing only when he saw the tip of something white sticking out from under the bedspread. Kneeling down, Nate pulled out the pack of papers, recognizing them immediately.

It was the same divorce papers he'd signed and left for her. It had broken a part of him to write his name on the line, but he'd done it because it was what she wanted. Perhaps she'd left the papers for him, knowing he'd come here looking for her. Nice parting gift.

His gaze traveled over the page, his brain not registering a key piece of information for a few moments. When he saw it, his heart leaped into his throat with excitement.

Annie's signature line was blank.

Despite what she'd said, there was hope. She did love him or she wouldn't have left the papers she'd fought so hard for behind.

Crumpling the pages in his hand, Nate turned and marched out of the room. He didn't know where Annie had gone, but this time he wouldn't let her get away. He'd track her to the ends of the earth if he had to.

He blazed through the casino, noticing no one and nothing but the path to the restricted area. His heart felt lighter with every step, the situation less grim as the elevator ascended to his suite.

When the elevator doors opened, Nate came to a sudden stop on the landing. He was surprised to find Gabe restraining a visibly pissed-off Tessa in his office. He knew she'd been released on bail that morning, but he certainly hadn't expected her to return so quickly to the scene of the crime.

"Where is my sister?" Her pale skin was bright red with anger. It looked odd against the fiery auburn of her hair.

"I have no idea. Annie apparently left the hotel after she was eliminated from the tournament. She's probably flying over Mississippi by now."

"She didn't leave, and she isn't answering her phone. That's not like her." Her blue eyes, so much like Annie's it made Nate's chest ache, widened with newfound fear. She tugged at Gabe's grip but this time the head of security let her go. "Jerry. He told me he would do something to her if I mentioned his involvement to the police. I didn't say anything, though. I knew I couldn't trust him."

"Jerry who?" Nate knew Tessa couldn't possibly be talking about the only Jerry he knew. He was in his seventies with a heart condition. There was no way he'd hurt a hair on Annie's head, and if he tried, the stress would probably kill him. Annie never bent easily to anyone's will.

"*Casino manager* Jerry. He masterminded this whole thing. The bastard set me up so he could blackmail her into taking my place."

Nate had to take a moment to wrap his head around the idea of his grandfather's friend as a crook. "Take your place? Was she involved the whole time?"

"No, of course not. Don't you know Annie at all? She didn't get hauled into it until yesterday. It's all my fault."

The realization hit low to his gut. Yesterday. Everything had changed yesterday after Tessa was eliminated. If Annie had been forced into taking Tessa's place...that was why she'd left. Why she'd said it didn't matter how she felt about him because it didn't change anything. And he'd turned around and signed the divorce papers. He'd fallen for her bluff and now she was in danger.

"Would he hurt her?"

Tessa bit her lip and nodded. "Both Jerry and Eddie have guns. They never got physical with me, but the threat was always there. If they feel like their plan has fallen apart, they just might do anything."

The loud beep of Nate's cell phone chirped at his hip. He pressed the radio button and yelled, "Not now," into the receiver. It didn't matter who it was or what was wrong at the casino. Right now, only Annie and her safety mattered.

"Yes, now." It was Jerry's demanding voice that echoed in the room. "Turn your radio to channel five."

Channel five was almost never used, and when it was, it was for private conversations. Nate clicked over. "I'm here."

"You and your wife have ruined all my plans and owe me a lot of money to make up for what I've lost. But I'm giving you a chance to fix it. You're going to come to my hotel suite with a duffel bag filled with ten million dollars. You're going to come alone and you're not going to involve the police or hotel security."

Nate looked quickly to Gabe, who nodded in encouragement, staying silent. "And why, exactly, would I do that, Jerry?"

The old man chuckled over the static of the walkie-talkie connection. "There's an envelope on your desk. Open it."

Nate crossed the room to his desk and found the unmarked envelope setting on his blotter. It hadn't been there earlier. Inside, he found Annie's wedding ring. "If you hurt her..." he began, but didn't get to finish his threat.

"I don't intend to hurt her as long as you do what I say. I intend to get my money and set her free. You've got one hour. And remember, I'm monitoring the in-house communications system. If so much as a whisper about this comes up, Annie's dead."

The connection ended. Nate dropped the phone and the ring to the desk, bracing his hands on the wood to help him keep control of his anger.

"He didn't count on me being here," Gabe said. "We have the advantage."

"What do we do?" Tessa asked.

"We're going to do what he asked. I want you to stay

here," he said to Tessa, then turned to Gabe. "We'll have one of your guys sit with her up here. I want you to come with me."

"What do you need me to do?" Gabe was at his side in an instant, his years of strategic military experience finally being put to good use.

"I need you to give me your gun."

Annie had one hell of a headache.

She'd woken in a dark room, realizing fairly quickly that she was handcuffed to a hotel headboard. The metal cuffs were digging painfully into her wrists, and the movement made her stomach swim with nausea.

Turning her head, she could see the light coming under the doorway. Muffled voices were outside, but she couldn't tell who it was. She didn't need to be a detective to decide she was in Jerry's suite. The room had the same old smell of cigarettes and industrial cleaner, and she could hear children splashing and playing in the courtyard pool she'd noticed outside his window the day before.

She should've taken Jerry's threats more seriously. Somehow she'd believed that if she was out of the tournament and Tessa was safe in police custody, he'd no longer have control over her life. She'd been painfully mistaken.

Now she would pay. She didn't know how, but Jerry would punish her for her impudence. The idea was frightening, but a part of Annie had accepted this outcome the moment she'd chosen to throw the tournament. She'd retaken control of her life. If this was the price she paid, she only had one regret: that the last thing she ever said to Nate was a lie spoken in anger. He might never know the truth about how she felt.

The voices outside the door grew louder as they came

closer. Annie braced herself for their arrival, struggling to sit up and put her back against the headboard. She might not have the use of her hands, but she could move her legs and by God, she'd make sure none of them would ever breed.

When the door opened, Annie could see the outline of two men in the doorway. One was Jerry, she could tell by the bald dome of his head and the slouch of his aged posture. The second was Eddie. The light illuminated the stupid Cowboys jacket he always wore. She'd expected him to be in Atlantic City by now.

"Sleeping Beauty is awake," Jerry said, flipping on the light and temporarily blinding Annie.

"Now the fun begins." Eddie's mouth twisted into an evil grin as he crossed the room. He reached out to touch Annie's face but jerked away when the cold slime of her spit landed on his cheek.

"You don't touch me," she warned, but her bravado was short-lived. Eddie's hand flew at her face. The impact exploded across her cheek in a fierce wave of pain.

Eddie leaned in, his breath hot and rancid on her face. "Try that again and you and your sister will both regret it."

"I thought you'd be long gone by now, Eddie. You've always been too chicken to do the dirty work yourself." Annie prepared herself for another slap, but Jerry pulled Eddie back before his fist could fly again.

"We don't have time for that. Go in the other room," he demanded and watched Eddie slink out. "You are a hellcat, Annie. I never quite know what to expect from you. Makes me wish I was thirty years younger. You'd be a fun one to break." He sighed, returning to the doorway. "Instead, I'll just have to break Nate and let you watch. He should be here soon with the money he owes me."

"Money?"

"Ten million dollars in exchange for you. That's more than I would've made in the tournament, so I think it's a fair trade. Enough to get me out of this godforsaken town and afford me the lifestyle I deserve after nearly killing myself for this casino."

"I wouldn't be so sure he'll show up with the money," Annie said. A part of her prayed he would save her while another hoped her words were true. She didn't want to be the bait they used to trap him. Even if Nate brought the money, she didn't believe Jerry would just hand her over and stroll out of the hotel. "I did a pretty good job of pushing him away, thanks to you. We're getting a divorce. He may not care what you do with me."

"Oh, he cares, Annie." Jerry flipped off the light and pulled the door closed behind him. "I'd bet ten million on it."

The thirty minutes it had taken to get things in place had felt like hours. By the time Nate started down the hallway to Jerry's office, the adrenaline was pumping so furiously through his veins he was tempted to break down the door instead of using his master key.

But he was determined to stick to his plan. He shifted the duffel bag in his hands, checked on the gun in his suit coat pocket then slipped the key into the lock. The door swung open wide, his gaze sweeping the room until it locked in on his target. His hand slipped into his pocket, his fingers tightening around the grip of the gun.

Jerry was sitting at his desk, alone. As always, he was surrounded by paperwork, the space reminding Nate so much of how it looked when he was a kid visiting his grandfather. The betrayal of a family friend was still a bitter pill for him to swallow.

His target barely moved; his gaze focused intently on Nate without a hint of surprise. Jerry stood slowly, his hands held up to show Nate he was unarmed. "I'm glad you finally made it, Nate. We've been waiting for you."

"Where is she?"

Jerry gave a condescending smile and came out from behind his desk. "Close by and feisty as ever, I assure you."

Nate swallowed hard. He hoped it was true, but he wouldn't take Jerry's word for it. "I want to see her."

"Or what? Are you going to use that gun in your pocket to shoot your grandfather's oldest and dearest friend? The man who's worked with you and helped you make this hotel a success? Come now, we both know that isn't going to happen, so why don't you just relax and have a seat." Jerry took a step toward Nate, his hand held out to gesture toward the seating area.

Nate didn't move from his spot. "What is this all about, Jerry? Money?"

"What's wrong with it being about money? It makes the world go round. You of all people should know that."

"Are you in some kind of trouble? Do you owe someone money?" Nate struggled to find a reason why Jerry would do something like this.

"That's how it started, yes. I do have a fondness for the ponies but not much of an eye for picking a winner. I ran through all my retirement savings pretty quickly, which is why I came back to work. I got in with an interesting crowd when I couldn't pay the bookies what I owed. Fixing poker tournaments started as a way to get them off my back, but I soon realized there were bigger payoffs and bigger thrills in this game."

"Of all the people you could've chosen, why Tessa?

Why my Annie? Were you trying to get back at me for something I did?"

"Not really. We chose Tessa because she was young, stupid and could lead us to Annie. She was our real target in the end. If she met with great success, no one would ever suspect. It was a perfect plan. I didn't realize at the time that she was your wife. It was quite the pleasant surprise when I found out the two of you were coming together to catch the cheaters. I knew every move you made because you told Gabe and me everything."

"Did you really think Annie would be so pliable?"

Jerry laughed. "No, but everyone has a button you can push. Apply the right kind of pressure and you can make a woman madly in love betray her husband and sabotage her own career."

She did love him. It made Nate sick to think of how Annie had come to him at Jerry's demand. "How'd that work out for you?"

Jerry shrugged. "It worked great until Annie started crumbling under the pressure. She couldn't have won a game of Go Fish with the way she was mooning at you over her cards. She completely lost her focus. There wasn't a damn thing we could do to salvage her game. The two of you ruined all my plans. The polite thing to do—" he gestured toward the duffel bag with a smile "—is to make it up to me."

"Well, here it is," Nate said through angrily gritted teeth. He wanted to drop the bag and pistol-whip the old man, but he couldn't until he knew Annie was safe. "Where's Annie? I want to see her first."

Jerry sighed and shook his head. "You seem to be working under the impression that you're calling the shots. You're just like your grandfather, thinking you're in control of everything when it's people like me that make you successful. Give me the damn bag. And the gun."

"Not until I see her."

Before Jerry could answer, the bedroom door flew open and Eddie came in, dragging Annie with him. He held a gun to her head and had his arm wrapped around her neck in a chokehold. Seeing her like that made something primitive rise up inside Nate. It took everything he had not to pull out his gun and shoot Eddie on the spot. Unfortunately, he was not a marksman, and with Annie furiously struggling in Eddie's arms, Nate couldn't be certain not to hit her instead.

"So you've seen her. She's obviously still got some fight left in her. So put down the gun and the money and step away."

Nate ignored Jerry and took a few steps to the right toward Annie. Confused by his movement, Eddie dragged her back toward the window and away from Nate's approach.

"The money and the gun, Nate. Now."

Eddie nervously pulled back the hammer on the gun. Nate couldn't trust him not to shoot Annie, even if by accident.

"Okay, okay," he said, easing the gun down onto the floor and kicking it toward Jerry. "Please stop pointing the gun at her."

"After I get the money," Jerry said. The old man bent over to pick up the gun.

The rest happened in a blur. Nate yelled, "Now!" A loud bang rang out. Annie screamed. Nate swung the duffel bag filled with poker chips at Jerry, the heavy and unexpected blow knocking him to the ground. Nate quickly scooped up the gun. He held it on Jerry, his eyes darting back to the shattered window. Annie stood there alone, her entire body trembling in shock and fear as she tried to process what had happened.

The door burst open and a dozen men in navy security uniforms rushed into the room. Once they had Jerry in custody, Nate dropped his gun and ran to Annie's side. He crushed her against him, tugging her away from Eddie, who was howling in pain at her feet.

Gabe's sniper training had served them well today. With Nate's cell phone on in his pocket the entire time, Gabe had waited patiently across the hotel courtyard for Eddie to get into position and Nate to give the order to shoot. His bullet had crossed the distance and found its mark in Eddie's shoulder.

Nate pulled Annie from the suite, taking her far away from the scene of her captivity. She didn't speak, just cried against the lapel of his jacket until they reached the empty hotel room they'd set aside when they'd planned their attack. He sat Annie on the bed and wrapped her shoulders with a thick blanket.

"You're going to be okay," he whispered into her hair, gently stroking her back. "Gabe's calling the police, and the ambulance should be here soon. They'll take good care of you, okay?"

"I don't want a divorce."

Annie's voice was so small Nate wasn't quite sure he heard her correctly. "What did you say?"

Annie pulled away, gently brushing her tears from her cheek. She winced in pain as she moved, making Nate's chest ache. If Jerry rotted in jail ten years after he was dead, it wouldn't be long enough to make up for what he'd done.

"I said I don't want a divorce."

"We don't have to talk about that right now. You've been through a lot."

"No, we do. I've already waited too long and almost missed my chance to say it. I hate myself for what I said to you. Jerry made me do it, and it just broke my heart. I lied to you, Nate. I do love you. I always have, I was just too scared to say it. After today, I realize there are so many other things in life to fear than love. Tonight, all I could think about was that I might die without telling you how I really felt. That you might always think those horrible things I said to you were true."

"Annie, I—"

"Let me finish," she interrupted. "I don't know how to be a wife, and I can't always promise I'll be a good one, but I want to spend the rest of my life with you trying to figure it out. If you still want me, I'd love to plant roots here in Vegas and travel with you by my side."

Nate couldn't help but smile. His heart was leaping in his chest. "If I still want you? Annie, I've never stopped wanting you from the moment I first laid eyes on you. I love you. More than anything." Nate hugged her gently against him and pressed a soft kiss to her lips. "Don't ever believe otherwise."

They sat in silence for a few minutes, letting the truth of their words and the gravity of the situation they'd just experienced fully sink in. Nate could hear the police going up and down the hallway and Gabe's voice ordering the staff around. It wouldn't be long before their moment together would be disrupted by police interviews and EMT examinations.

"So you really think we can do this whole marriage thing?" Annie asked at last.

Nate sighed and leaned his head against hers. "I think we can have a great marriage. One you'll want to run to instead of run from."

Epilogue

Annie could feel the Caribbean sun's rays sinking warmly into her bones. The combination of the heat and the rum was doing wonders for her state of mind. She needed this. After the shooting, she'd decided to take a break from the game. It seemed like a good idea to get away from the chaos and noise of the casino and the game that had ruled her life for so long.

Once the scandal with Jerry broke and hit the news, it became abundantly clear she wasn't going to get any peace in Las Vegas. On ESPN they were constantly showing pictures of her next to Tessa's, Eddie's and Jerry's mug shots.

Nate had decided they both needed to get away from the Sapphire and turned over the running of the hotel to his new casino manager. They'd spent some time at the house in Henderson, then visited his father in Texas. After that, Nate had suggested a few weeks on St. Thomas at the family beach house. They'd only been there a few days, but she had to say this whole vacation thing was pretty damn great. She'd have to make a point to schedule more of these in between tournaments and time in Vegas with Nate.

Annie took a sip of her drink and closed her eyes. This was the way to live. She was feeling so good nothing could ruin her buzz.

"I was thinking we should get remarried when Tessa gets out on parole."

Almost nothing. Annie rolled onto her side on the queen-size lounge chair. Nate was lying beside her, absentmindedly thumbing at the keypad of his smartphone. Getting him to take a vacation was a big step, although she was doing better at the actual vacationing part so far.

"Remarried? Did I miss the part where we divorced?"

"I mean like a vow renewal or something. Have a reception. Some cake. We could let our families and friends come this time."

Annie sighed and considered the idea of a real wedding. Their first had been such a blur. They'd rushed through it, so anxious to just be married that she hadn't relished the details the way a woman normally wanted to. She hadn't been raised dreaming about her wedding day like other little girls. And yet even there the tides had turned.

When she'd called her mother to tell her about Tessa's unfortunate incarceration, Magdala Baracas announced quite suddenly that she'd gotten married to her Portuguese businessman. The change of heart probably meant that not only would her mother and uh…*stepfather*… come to the wedding, they might even enjoy themselves. This was new territory for the Baracas women.

"Would we have it at the hotel?" The Desert Sapphire had a very nice wedding chapel. They'd made quick use of it the first time.

"No, I think we should do it here."

"St. Thomas?"

"Yeah. We could get married on the beach at sunset. I'll have some of the locals build us a gazebo. We could have a bonfire and eat seafood until we throw up."

"Sounds lovely," Annie said, her tone flat with sarcasm.

Nate put down his phone and rolled over to face her. "I'm being serious here. Barbara Ann Baracas Reed, would you do me the honor of marrying me again with our friends and family as witnesses?"

Annie opened her mouth to answer when Nate pulled a small velvet box from his shorts. "What is that?"

He frowned. "That is not the appropriate response." When he flipped open the box, Annie was nearly blinded by the large, heart-shaped diamond ring inside.

"You never got a diamond before. I thought you deserved one now." Nate pulled the ring from the box and slipped it onto Annie's finger next to her wedding band.

Annie couldn't tear her eyes from it. It was the most beautiful ring she'd ever seen. She didn't know what to say.

"Are you okay?"

She looked up to see Nate's dark eyes filled with concern. "I'm wonderful. Why?"

"The last time I did this you passed out on me."

Annie had to laugh. Her world had turned on its end since that day. In a month's time, things had changed so dramatically it surprised even her. As she looked down at her new ring, there were no nerves, no butterflies. No screams from generations past urging her to run away. Nate's love had slain the dragons. Such an achievement should be celebrated. A wedding on the beach with too much seafood was a good place to start.

"Yes, Nate." She smiled, leaning in to place a kiss on his full, piña-colada-flavored lips. "I will marry you again. And again. And again."

* * * * *

*Don't miss these other stories from
Andrea Laurence:*

*WHAT LIES BENEATH
MORE THAN HE EXPECTED
UNDENIABLE DEMANDS
A BEAUTY UNCOVERED*

All available now from Harlequin Desire!

COMING NEXT MONTH FROM

HARLEQUIN®

Desire

Available March 4, 2014

#2287 THE REAL THING
The Westmorelands • by Brenda Jackson
To help Dr. Trinity Matthews fend off unwanted advances at work, Adrian Westmoreland poses as her boyfriend. But when their pretend kisses turn serious, Adrian wants a chance at the real thing.

#2288 THE TEXAS RENEGADE RETURNS
Texas Cattleman's Club: The Missing Mogul
by Charlene Sands
After regaining his memories, rancher Alex del Toro is determined to reclaim the woman he loves—in spite of their families' interference. But then he learns she's been keeping a little secret....

#2289 DOUBLE THE TROUBLE
Billionaires and Babies • by Maureen Child
When his ex-wife falls ill, Colt King discovers he's the father of two adorable twins. Now this unsure father is falling in love all over again—with his ex *and* their babies!

#2290 SEDUCING HIS PRINCESS
Married by Royal Decree • by Olivia Gates
Seducing the princess is Mohab's biggest mission impossible. Overcoming past deceptions and present heartaches, he vows to take her from fake engagement to temporary marriage to...forever.

#2291 SUDDENLY EXPECTING
by Paula Roe
One night with his best friend, Sophie, and Marco Corelli can't get enough. Then, when they're trapped on his private island, Marco gets more than he expected...because Sophie's pregnant!

#2292 ONE NIGHT, SECOND CHANCE
The Hunter Pact • by Robyn Grady
After a sizzling one-night stand, Wynn Hunter is shocked to see his beautiful, nameless stranger again—and to learn exactly who she is! This time, he won't let her get away!

YOU CAN FIND MORE INFORMATION ON UPCOMING HARLEQUIN® TITLES, FREE EXCERPTS AND MORE AT WWW.HARLEQUIN.COM.

HDCNM0214

REQUEST YOUR FREE BOOKS!
2 FREE NOVELS PLUS 2 FREE GIFTS!

H HARLEQUIN®

Desire

ALWAYS POWERFUL, PASSIONATE AND PROVOCATIVE

YES! Please send me 2 FREE Harlequin Desire® novels and my 2 FREE gifts (gifts are worth about $10). After receiving them, if I don't wish to receive any more books, I can return the shipping statement marked "cancel." If I don't cancel, I will receive 6 brand-new novels every month and be billed just $4.55 per book in the U.S. or $4.99 per book in Canada. That's a savings of at least 13% off the cover price! It's quite a bargain! Shipping and handling is just 50¢ per book in the U.S. and 75¢ per book in Canada.* I understand that accepting the 2 free books and gifts places me under no obligation to buy anything. I can always return a shipment and cancel at any time. Even if I never buy another book, the two free books and gifts are mine to keep forever.

225/326 HDN F4ZC

Name _____ (PLEASE PRINT) _____

Address _____ Apt. # _____

City _____ State/Prov. _____ Zip/Postal Code _____

Signature (if under 18, a parent or guardian must sign)

Mail to the **Harlequin® Reader Service:**
IN U.S.A.: P.O. Box 1867, Buffalo, NY 14240-1867
IN CANADA: P.O. Box 609, Fort Erie, Ontario L2A 5X3

Want to try two free books from another line?
Call 1-800-873-8635 or visit www.ReaderService.com.

* Terms and prices subject to change without notice. Prices do not include applicable taxes. Sales tax applicable in N.Y. Canadian residents will be charged applicable taxes. Offer not valid in Quebec. This offer is limited to one order per household. Not valid for current subscribers to Harlequin Desire books. All orders subject to credit approval. Credit or debit balances in a customer's account(s) may be offset by any other outstanding balance owed by or to the customer. Please allow 4 to 6 weeks for delivery. Offer available while quantities last.

Your Privacy—The Harlequin® Reader Service is committed to protecting your privacy. Our Privacy Policy is available online at www.ReaderService.com or upon request from the Harlequin Reader Service.

We make a portion of our mailing list available to reputable third parties that offer products we believe may interest you. If you prefer that we not exchange your name with third parties, or if you wish to clarify or modify your communication preferences, please visit us at www.ReaderService.com/consumerschoice or write to us at Harlequin Reader Service Preference Service, P.O. Box 9062, Buffalo, NY 14269. Include your complete name and address.

HD13R

Let the show begin, Adrian thought as he stared deep into Trinity's eyes. He could sense her nervousness. Although she had gone along with her sister's suggestion that they pretend to be lovers, he had a feeling she wasn't 100 percent on board with the idea.

Although the man Trinity was trying to avoid was going about it all wrong, Adrian could understand Dr. Belvedere wanting her. Hell, what man in his right mind wouldn't? Trinity was an incredibly beautiful woman. *Ravishing* didn't even come close to describing her.

He recalled the reaction of almost every single man in the room when Trinity had shown up at Riley's wedding. That was when he'd heard she would be moving to Denver for two years to work at a local hospital.

"Are you sure it's him?" Trinity asked, breaking into his thoughts.

"Pretty positive," Adrian said, studying her features. She had creamy mahogany-colored skin, silky black hair that hung to her shoulders and the most gorgeous pair of light brown eyes he'd ever seen. "And it's just the way I planned it," he said.

She raised an arched brow. "The way you planned it?"

"Yes. After your sister called and told me about her idea, I decided to get on it right away. I found out from a reliable source that Belvedere frequents this place, especially on Thursday nights."

"So that's why you suggested we have dinner here tonight?" she asked.

"Yes, that's the reason. The plan is for him to see us together, right?"

"Yes. I just wasn't prepared to run into him tonight. Hopefully, all it will take is for him to see us together and—"

"Back off? Don't bank on that. The man wants you and, for some reason, he feels he has every right to have you. Getting him to leave you alone won't be easy. We should really do something to get his attention."

"What?"

"Just follow my lead."

And then Adrian leaned in and kissed her lips.

Will this pretend relationship turn into something real?
Find out in
THE REAL THING
by New York Times *and* USA TODAY *bestselling author*
Brenda Jackson
Available March 2014
Only from Harlequin® Desire

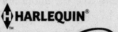

HARLEQUIN®
Desire

ALWAYS POWERFUL, PASSIONATE AND PROVOCATIVE.

**USA TODAY bestselling author Olivia Gates
is back with a scorching tale of power and
passion, honor and love in her acclaimed
marriage-of-convenience series**

There is only one woman for Mohab Aal Ghaanem,
Saraya's top secret service agent. He lost her once,
but the promise of peace between two feuding kingdoms
could bring Jala Aal Masood back to him—as his wife.

Marry *Mohab?* Six years ago, the Saraya prince risked his life
to save Jala's. He awoke irresistible desire…only to destroy her
trust. Now royal decree commands the Judar princess make
the ultimate sacrifice by giving herself to Mohab. Will fresh
heartbreak be her destiny? Or is this her second chance with
the man she never stopped loving?

Look for
SEDUCING HIS PRINCESS next month,
from Harlequin® Desire!

Wherever books and ebooks are sold.

Don't miss other scandalous titles from the
Married by Royal Decree miniseries, available now!

TEMPORARILY HIS PRINCESS
by Olivia Gates

CONVENIENTLY HIS PRINCESS
by Olivia Gates

HARLEQUIN®

Desire

ALWAYS POWERFUL, PASSIONATE AND PROVOCATIVE.

What happens in Vegas…

It had been years since Colton King ended his marriage to Penny Oaks. He'd declared their whirlwind Las Vegas nuptials over after just one day. The dedicated businessman had tried to erase her from his memory. Then he discovered Penny had been keeping a huge secret. Actually two little secrets—a baby boy and a baby girl.

Now this unsure father is falling in love all over again—is he prepared to prove he can be all she needs?

Look for DOUBLE THE TROUBLE
by Maureen Child next month.

Don't miss other scandalous titles from the
Billionaires and Babies miniseries, available now!

YULETIDE BABY SURPRISE
by Catherine Mann

CLAIMING HIS OWN
by Elizabeth Gates

A BILLIONAIRE FOR CHRISTMAS
by Janice Maynard

THE NANNY'S SECRET
by Elizabeth Lane

SNOWBOUND WITH A BILLIONAIRE
by Jules Bennett